Summer Waves

Volume I

Ukiyoto Publishing

All global publishing rights are held by

Ukiyoto Publishing

Published in 2022

Content Copyright © Ukiyoto

ISBN 9789364944939

All rights reserved.
No part of this publication may be reproduced, transmitted, or stored in a retrieval system, in any form by any means, electronic, mechanical, photocopying, recording or otherwise, without the prior permission of the publisher.

The moral rights of the author have been asserted.

This is a work of fiction. Names, characters, businesses, places, events, locales, and incidents are either the products of the author's imagination or used in a fictitious manner. Any resemblance to actual persons, living or dead, or actual events is purely coincidental.

This book is sold subject to the condition that it shall not by way of trade or otherwise, be lent, resold, hired out or otherwise circulated, without the publisher's prior consent, in any form of binding or cover other than that in which it is published.

"And so with the sunshine and the great bursts of leaves growing on the trees, just as things grow in fast movies, I had that familiar conviction that life was beginning over again with the summer."

- F. Scott Fitzgerald, The Great Gatsby

Contents

Short Story by Kiran Hiwale	1
Short Story by Santhini Govindan	9
Short Story by S P Singh	22
Short Story by Priyanka Joshi More	44
Poem by Indrani Chowdhury	76
Short Story by Kuntala Bhattacharya	81
Short Story by Chinmay Chakravarty	103
Poem by Deep Wilson	110
Essay by Srividya Muthuvel	134
About the Authors	144

Short Story by Kiran Hiwale

Changing Past for a Better Future

13ᵗʰ April 2022

*"Mohe tu rang de basanti, Yaara,
Mohe tu rang de basanti!"*

(Song lyrics: Colour me saffron, o friend, colour me saffron!)

Tears rolled down Kranti's eyes as she watched the patriotic movie on TV. Suddenly she heard a big thud on the bungalow's porch. A huge Jeep, like a military vehicle, stood there. The driver's door opened, and Veer, her husband, peeped out. He waved at her with joy and shouted, "It's working now!"

"Wow! Incredible!" She ran to him.

"Now, this is our ticket to anywhere!" Veer's eyes were beaming with a sense of accomplishment, "Tell me time & Place, and this will take us there!"

"I want to go to Jallianwala Bagh and stop the massacre from happening."

"Jallianwala Bagh? What else could I expect from a history professor!" Veer shook his head in disbelief! "Won't you like to go to the future and check what amazing technology exists? Or travel to the past and watch Elvis Presley's live performance?"

"This is your groundbreaking invention! Instead of using it just as a tourist car, we should go back, prevent the worst incidents in the past to make an even more wonderful future!"

"Changing a historical event can be complicated! But we can try. Come inside!"

13ᵗʰ April 1919 04:00 pm

Veer's Jeep appeared at the entrance of Jallianwala Bagh with the thud. Veer and Kranti stepped out. People stared at their outfits. Kranti wore a green dress, and Veer was in a blue t-shirt and navy jeans.

People of all age groups were celebrating the Baisakhi festival in the park. Freedom fighters had erected a stage for cultural performances and political speeches. Veer asked for the mike to sing a patriotic song and the unsuspecting organiser obliged.

Veer played the music from Kranti's iPhone and started singing. Kranti started dancing in Punjabi style. Surprised people began paying attention to them.

"Ding ding ding ding ding ding ding

Thodi si dhul meri, Dharti ki mere watan ki

Thodisi khushbu, Baurai se mast pavan ki"

(Song lyrics: Some dust from the soil of my nation, Some fragrance of crazily wild wind!)

After grabbing everyone's attention, Veer gave the mike to Kranti.

"Brothers and Sisters, you are surprised with this music and song, aren't you? This song is from the future, from a patriotic movie *Rang De Basanti,* made in 2006. Our country got the freedom that you are fighting for on 15th August 1947. However, today a tragedy will take place if you stay here. General Dyer is coming with his armed unit and going to open fire on all of you. Leave this park immediately, or you will die!"

People were shocked and started running towards the exit. The event organiser snatched the mic from Kranti.

"Listen, everyone! Don't let this costume player trick you! General Dyer can't open fire on unarmed women and kids! At most, there will be a lathi-charge that we should face with the spirit of Satyagraha for the release of our leaders."

The volunteers pushed the couple away from the stage.

Most men decided to stay while women rushed to exit with children.

Kranti held her head in both hands, "Oh my God! Am I going to witness the massacre in person?"

"The casualties will be less," Veer consoled." Let's get out of here, or we won't be able to go back!"

Veer took her back to the Jeep, where General Dyer's armed vehicle with a machine gun had already arrived.

"Whose car is this?" Dyer shouted.

"It's mine, general!" Veer said. "This isn't a normal car; it's a time machine! We came from the future year 2021."

"If you kill these people today, you will face disciplinary action and will be relieved of your command on 23rd March 1920," Kranti added.

"What rubbish! I am going to teach them a lesson they will never forget."

"Don't believe us? Look at this gadget from the future," Veer opened the rear door of the car. Dyer peeped inside, and before he could understand what was happening, Veer pushed him inside and closed the door. Then he jumped into the driving seat.

The soldiers ran towards the Jeep but thud! It vanished!

15th October 1997

"Open the car door, or I will shoot you!" Dyer shouted.

"Fine!" Veer obliged.

Dyer got confused when he stepped out. The Jallianwala Bagh area looked different. The police that controlled the crowd looked different.

"We are in the year 1997, celebrating 50 years of independence from British rule. You can witness Queen Elizabeth II, granddaughter of your King George V, lay a wreath to pay homage to thousands of innocents you killed," Kranti explained.

"I am just trying to do my job to avoid a mutiny."

"But nobody, even from the British government, could justify the killing of thousands of unarmed innocents," Kranti explained to him the repercussions of the massacre in more detail.

"Okay, I got it. Drop me back!" He conceded.

13th April 1919 06:00 pm

Back at Jallianwala Bagh, Veer and Kranti watched Dyer as he maintained his strict façade, re-announced the curfew, and asked the crowd to disperse. When few freedom fighters remained, he ordered them arrested.

"See, future woman!" the organiser scorned Kranti, "I knew that Dyer won't fire!"

13ᵗʰ April 2022

On returning home, Veer googled "Jallianwala Bagh Massacre."

"Look at this! Only a normal description of the park but no mention of the massacre!"

"Yay! We avoided it!" Kranti hugged him with joy.

"What next?"

"I want to thwart the India-Pakistan partition!"

"Oh my God! Why can't you think of something joyful and exotic?"

With a crazy face, Veer googled "independence of India" and read aloud,

"India became a British Dominion in 1944. 1944? And gained full independence in 1961." He was confused. "What does it mean?"

"It means, without the Jallianwala Bagh Massacre and the outrage that followed, our freedom fighters accepted partial independence within the British Empire in 1944," Kranti explained and then panicked. "Oh, Sh*t! What else have we changed?"

Short Story by Santhini Govindan

The Lie That Grew

Matthew had not planned to tell the lie. He had not wanted to do so either. It was just that the lie, which had sounded so very right at the time, had sort of slipped off his tongue, as if by itself, before he could stop it. And once it was there, out in the open, a public pronouncement, there was nothing he could do to take it back. And in the days that followed, it was always there, lingering at the back of his mind, posing a threat to his peace, as he thought about all the damage it had the potential to do.

It had all started off quite innocently during the Moral Science period. Since it was the beginning of the school year, it was the time for introductions, and the class teacher had asked every student to say a few words about himself to the rest of the class. Each one could speak about their families or friends, hobbies and special interests, or anything that was important to them, which would give the rest of the class an idea of the kind of person they were. And as the students started speaking, one by one, Matthew, a shy diminutive boy, seated in the last row, felt his heart sink.

He was a "new" boy at this particular school, and it seemed to him that all the students led such full and interesting lives, and had varied and unusual interests and talents. There were ace amateur photographers and computer buffs, poets and guitarists, and singers. There were students who kept exotic pets, or had travelled to faraway lands Matthew had only heard of, and as he listened to these interesting accounts, he felt that he was a very dull person, and his life was very prosaic, and boring in comparison.

His father was a hard working banker, and his mother, a teacher at a local primary school. He had a ten-year-old sister, and the family lived in a small, neat apartment in a very crowded, middle class locality. Their daily lives, though busy, were crowded with common, everyday occurrences, and Matthews parents, who were always trying to balance their budget against rising costs, had neither the time, nor the finances, for what they called "exotic pastimes." Matthew liked to read, and play cricket in his spare time, but suddenly, he felt reluctant to speak about these very "ordinary," hobbies to his classmates.

He wished heartily that he had something really special, or spectacular to speak about, - something that would make everyone sit up and listen. He really wanted to be noticed! These regrets kept flitting through his mind, and then it was his turn to stand up.

"I am Matthew," he said hesitantly, after rising slowly to his feet. "I am really glad to be here as a new student of this school." And as he looked at all the eager, expectant faces turned towards him, he was seized by the inexplicable urge to boast, and show off! And the words that tumbled out of his mouth next, seemed to flow out of their own volition.

"I live in a large bungalow," he said, describing the gracious villa of old Colonel Pereira, which was overlooked by the apartment building where he lived. "It has a lovely garden that is full of all kinds of plants and flowers. My mother and I are keen gardeners. We have fruit trees too — guavas, chikoos, limes, mangoes, and papayas. I enjoy playing in the garden a lot, especially with my dog, Pongo."

Then Matthew described Pongo, who was a beautiful four-year-old Dalmatian dog, and the constant companion of Colonel Pereira. Matthew often stood on the balcony and watched him for long periods. He was a marvellous animal, very intelligent and disciplined. He knew lots of tricks too, and Matthew wanted very much to play with him, but Colonel Pereira, a crusty old bachelor, disliked small boys intensely, as they were always robbing the fruits and flowers from his garden. Matthew's overtures of friendship had been brusquely and abruptly rejected by the Colonel, and all Matthew ever got from him in return for his tentative smiles, were ferocious, forbidding glares. But Matthew continued to watch

Pongo longingly, and sometimes he made believe that the beautiful dog actually belonged to him!

So, as he spoke about Pongo to his class, he put all his secret fantasies into words. He described how Pongo greeted him rapturously everyday when he got home from school, and how he took him for long, rambling walks, and played "fetch" with him. With shining eyes, he told his class about the many tricks that Pongo could do, and what a good watchdog he was for the whole street. When Matthew had finished speaking, the rest of the class broke into spontaneous and enthusiastic applause, and Matthew sat down, face flushed with happiness and pride, at having become the centre of attention, and having made an impression!

The glow lasted all morning, and Matthew was on cloud nine until the recess, when the first stirrings of doubt over what he had done, presented themselves. He was surrounded by many boys; all asking more questions about his garden and dog Pongo.

As he answered each question, smiling widely, he heard a voice ask, "So, when can we come over to meet him? You said that he's very friendly! I'm sure that he would like it if you invite us over! We will all bring some goodies to share with him too! Just tell us what he likes!" Matthews's heart skipped a beat when he heard this, especially since everyone was looking expectantly at him. But there was hardly a tremor in his voice, as the next lie rolled off his tongue, as easily as the first one.

"I would love to invite all of you over, and I'm sure that Pongo would like it a lot too, but you see, right now there are some repairs going on at home, and it's not convenient to have friends over."

"Oh, that's okay," said one of the boys cheerfully. "We'll come over just as soon as the repairs are over! We'll remind you about it, Matthew, even if you forget!" Matthew heaved a sigh of relief at the reprieve he had got, but alas! It was not for long! Schoolboys have sharp memories for the things that they want, and within a week, several students were asking him anxiously whether the repairs to his house were over. "Not yet," he said, injecting the right amount of regret into his voice. Another week passed, and then ten days. By this time, the questions about the repairs to his "bungalow" were becoming more and more insistent, and to Matthew's over sensitive ears, they sounded rather doubtful and suspicious too.

And then, Matthew's lies, which seemed to have taken on a malevolent life of their own, grew again, as he glibly added another one to the already existing string.

"The repairs to the house are over at last," he told his classmates, feigning a huge, dramatic sigh of relief in their presence, "but there was so much dust and dirt all around the house during that time. It made my grandfather fall sick. My mother is so harassed right now, that I think that we will have to put off your visit for a few days..." The impatient boys had no choice but to accept this fresh excuse, but now Matthew was getting really worried and desperate. He had hoped that his account of his wonderful home and dog would quietly, and naturally fade away into the back of his classmates memories, or that his prevarication would put them off, but alas! His rather colourful account seemed to have really caught their imaginations. They were persistent in their desire to meet the "wonder dog Pongo," and Matthew was filled with panic and despair. He just could not hold his friends off for much longer, and he had no idea what he was going to do!

And then, unexpectedly a solution to Matthew's problem turned up. It was not by any means the ideal solution — in fact, when it was thrust upon Matthew, he was horrified and aghast, as he wondered how he would work it out. But as he had time to think about it slowly, it seemed to be the only way out of a very tricky situation! His class, Standard Eight, was having an Interclass Talent Competition and each of the four divisions had to put up a "Talent show," for the rest of the students to see and enjoy. The class with the best show would win a grand prize! A lively, animated discussion broke out in Matthew's class, Std. 8B, about what unusual items they could put up.

Matthew too was thinking hard, when suddenly, a boy pointed at him.

"Why, He can bring his dog Pongo for the show, and make him do some of his tricks. It will be the best item in the whole show...." he finished excitedly.

"Yes, yes!" cried the whole class in unison, absolutely thrilled with this novel idea.

"But...but animals are not allowed in school..." stammered an appalled Matthew, standing up, and looking anxiously at his teacher. But the teacher smiled indulgently at Matthew.

"Animals aren't usually allowed in school, but we will make an exception this time! Pongo can come to take part in our Talent Show."

"Hurray!" shouted the class excitedly, as Matthew with a weak and watery smile, sat down in his place.

And then what followed were discussions and still more discussions, among the students of Matthew's class about the Talent Show. As Matthew and "his" dog Pongo were given star billing, Matthew thought long and hard about how he would bring Colonel Pereira's dog to school on the day of the show. He had seen the Colonel make the dog do his tricks many a time, so he was quite confident of making him perform. And at last, he had, what he thought, was a foolproof plan to snatch the dog....

The day of the Contest dawned. Matthew got up quite early, and was dressed and ready much earlier than usual. He gulped down his breakfast, and hurried to the door.

"Why are you leaving so early, Matthew?" his mother asked him with a little frown.

"Today is our Talent Contest," he said. "I have to reach school early to help in the arrangements...." He stepped out of the gates of his apartment building, and set off at a brisk pace. He crossed the Colonel's house nonchalantly, and as he did so, he smiled in satisfaction. Colonel Pereira was in a corner of his large verandah practising his morning yoga as usual, with his eyes shut. His dog Pongo was sniffing around in the large garden. Matthew ducked behind a tree just beyond the Colonel's house, and quickly took out a small paper bag from his school bag. It was full of choice tidbits that he had gathered over the previous two days — chocolates, cakes, biscuits, and he quickly and soundlessly tiptoed upto the Colonels gate, and held out the bag through the bars of the gate.

Pongo picked up the scent of all the goodies that were usually forbidden to him at once, and with tail wagging and nose twitching, trotted eagerly to the gate. And from then on, it was a cinch for Matthew to spirit him away. As the big dog fell upon the bag slobbering, he opened the gate and slipped a rope through his collar, and before the surprised dog could even say, "BOW!" he and Matthew were running at full speed towards the school. What a sensation they caused when they reached school! Students and staff surrounded the beautiful spotted dog. As Matthew basked in all the praise and attention, he felt that all his lies might actually have been worth it after all!

The talent show began soon after, and as Matthew took the stage with Pongo, there was a storm of applause. Matthew beamed, and held up a biscuit.

"Now I will make Pongo beg for this biscuit," he said loudly. But when he turned to the dog, he found that the animal, frightened and bewildered by the strange and noisy place he found himself in, had backed into a corner of the stage, and stood there growling menacingly. Matthew's heart sank, but he kept his voice steady as he called out the dog's name, and held out the biscuit. A hush fell over the audience, and then, without any warning Pongo dashed across the stage with the speed of lightning, leapt out through an open window, and escaped! As pandemonium broke out, Matthew dashed out behind him into the school compound in hot pursuit, but it was of no use. The big dog was long gone...

As he returned to the school building later, completely crestfallen, his concerned teacher was waiting for him.

"You had better go home immediately Matthew," she said, "and find out whether your dog has reached home. Dogs usually find their way back very quickly..." Slowly, Matthew walked back towards his home, and as he neared the Colonel's house, his heart sank. It was surrounded by police cars, and the Colonel himself, very red in the face, was standing at the gate, gesticulating and shouting.

"I am telling you that he has not just gone out for a walk!" he bellowed. "He is the most obedient and well trained dog! He is a very valuable animal too! I tell you, he has been stolen from me..." His voice choked on his words, as he thought of his missing pet, and as Matthew saw the sorrow and despair in his face, his feet went towards him, as if on their own volition.

"Sir," he said very quietly and fearfully, barely looking at the colonel. The Colonel looked at him impatiently.

"Yes?" he barked. "What do you want?"

"It's about your—your dog..." stammered Matthew.

"Yes? What do you know about him?" asked the Colonel, hope kindling in his eyes.

"Well, it's like this. I have a talent contest...and... Oh.I took him to school...." he finally blurted out. There was an incredulous silence and then the Colonel sprang forward and roared, "You did what?" And then as the whole sorry story was revealed, and the Colonel grew angrier and angrier, Matthew, unable to contain himself, burst into tears!

"Now, Now," said one of the policemen kindly, leading the way to the police car." There's no need to be so upset! Since we know where you took the dog, we can easily find him. He can't have gone too far..."

"I don't know about that," said the Colonel darkly. But before they could get into the car, there was an excited woof and Pongo himself came bounding along the pavement with tongue hanging out. He hurled himself upon his master with great joy and excitement and the gruff old Colonel also threw his arms around the great black and white dog. Matthew heaved a huge sigh of relief, and tried to slink away quietly, but the Colonel wasn't letting him go that easily!

He reached out and pulled Matthew back by his shoulder.

"And as for you young man," he said sternly, "I'm wondering what I am going to do with you!" Matthew shivered and closed his eyes. Then, unexpectedly, the Colonel laughed. Matthew's eyes flew open and met the twinkling eyes of the Colonel.

"I think you have learnt your lesson," he said. "So you may stay and play with Pongo for a while, if you like. Your school must be over for the day." And as Matthew looked at the lovely big dog, wagging his tail enthusiastically, he was sorely tempted to agree with this last statement, rather than to go back to school to face his angry classmates. But he checked himself in time.

"No thank you," he said politely. "Perhaps some other time. I have to go back to school." Matthew had learnt his lesson. Never again would he tell a lie! For lies, have a habit of growing.

Short Story by S P Singh

The Two Faces of Summer

On a sweltering summer evening, the platform number four of the New Delhi Railway Station was jam-packed with passengers, their friends and relatives who were there to see them off. They all waited for The Ranikhet Express to move out. The train whistled a few times. The green signal was on, but the guard, in a faded dress, chatted with his friends. He showed no urgency. Some passengers sat in their seats while others, who knew how the railway functioned, waited on the platform in needless anxiety. A few travellers shopped for the books, magazines, snacks, tea and bottled water. The latecomers with coolies in tow rushed towards the train and searched for their seats.

Finally, the driver's patience ran out, and the train moved with a long, shrill whistle. Amid pandemonium, the passengers on the platform ran inside, pushing through the people and inviting their angry stares.

"Thank God! The train's late; otherwise I'd have missed it today. Delhi has so much population that you face traffic jams everywhere," a woman in mid-thirties mumbled, and then yelled at the coolie, "*Bhaiya*, berth 32 is here. Get the luggage fast. The train's moving."

"I've reservation for A 32," the latecomer said to the woman sitting on that seat.

"Yeah, it's yours. Mine is the upper one," the woman said, and shifted to the opposite berth, making room for her.

"Take this," the latecomer said, handing a fifty-rupee note to the coolie.

"Thank you, memsahib." The coolie pocketed the money and jumped out.

Within a few minutes, the train picked up speed and left the city lights behind. It was 9 p.m. Lateness of the train by fifteen minutes had enabled her to board it on time. Through the tinted, unclean windows of the air-conditioned coupe, both the women, with mixed feelings, watched the darkness swallow the city. They were escaping from Delhi for different reasons. One was returning home to join her husband in Nainital, while the other was going to her mother in Ranikhet after fighting with her husband. After a while, they looked at each other, exchanged smiles and got into conversation.

"I'm Divya." The first woman extended her hand and felt the co-passenger's hand soft and sweaty.

"I'm Shivani. Shivani Rawat. That's my maiden name I kept after my marriage despite my husband's objection," said the second woman, who had boarded the moving train.

Then both fell silent for a moment.

"I'm going to Nainital to join my husband. I'd come to Delhi to look up my ailing aunt," said Shivani and then put her hand in the handbag and fished out a hand mirror, hair clip and lipstick. She pulled her hair back and put on the clip. Then she retouched her lips, a lighter shade of brown, and replaced the items in the bag. A stolen glance at the co-passenger gave her delight and relief. But Divya's gaze a second later forced her to hide her triumphant grin.

Later, she pulled her legs up on the seat and made herself comfortable. They were the only passengers in that coupe, meant for four, and it gave them confidence as the other two seats were vacant. After a while, in walked the travelling ticket examiner wearing crumpled white trousers, black coat faded at the elbows and collar, and a black tie. He matched their tickets with the chart, glanced at their IDs and asked them to be alert as only a few women were travelling in that compartment. They fumed in indignation at his casual remark on an important issue of women's safety.

"Where do you live in Nainital?" asked Divya.

"My house is a furlong from Naina Devi Temple. My hubby is a writer. Presently, he is writing about the lost tribes of Kumaon. The book keeps him busy," Shivani spoke with a tinge of sadness in her eyes.

"Do you have kids?"

"Yeah, a son. He is in boarding school."

Then they shared a brief silence.

"Don't you think the writers are so different from others? I meant no pun for your husband." Divya broke the silence.

"Yeah, you're right. They are dreamers and often lost on their own. Often, it becomes quite unsettling," Shivani said with a faint smile. Then she gazed into Divya's eyes and asked, "Your hubby?"

"He is an exporter. Ours is a garment business," Divya replied.

"Isn't it great being married to a millionaire? One doesn't have to worry about money like a middle-class housewife. I heard the rich men are fun-loving, too." Shivani's eyes sparkled as she spoke.

"Yeah, but money is not everything. It's just a necessity. My hubby is more fun-loving than I can handle." Divya hid her anguish behind her smile.

"I beg to differ. Money is important to those who don't have enough of it," Shivani said.

"Maybe, but to those who have too much of it, it ceases to have any significance."

"That's the irony of life. Isn't it?"

"True."

Then they unpacked the paranthas, vegetables, and pickles, and shared the food. They craved for hot tea but at that late hour it was difficult to get as the next station was faraway and the train had no pantry car. So, they curbed their urge.

Putting the leftover in the plastic bag, they stood up and threw it in the dustbin. Shivani returned to the coupe. Divya went to the toilet. Since neither of them felt sleepy, they resumed their conversation.

Divya, the more talkative of the two, took the lead and asked Shivani, "How is life with a writer? I mean, how exciting it is."

"It's okay, sometimes thrilling but often boring. After a few years, the romance goes out of the marriage. I guess it's the same with every couple." Shivani took a deep sigh.

"I think it's so romantic for a woman to have someone write poetry for her, give her a poem and not flowers on her birthdays. It's so different, so out of the world," Divya said with a glint in her eyes.

"Yeah, once in a while, it's a heady feeling, but women like to be pampered with clothes and jewellery." Shivani winked.

"True, but the ornaments have no real meaning in life. To me, an honest relationship is more important," Divya said.

"What do you mean?"

"Being honest with each other and not cheating your spouse by sleeping around," Divya clarified.

"Is it an issue in today's world? Adultery is common even in small towns and cities. How can one keep a check when both the spouses travel often for work and deal with the opposite sex every day? It's human to succumb to the temptation." Shivani shrugged her shoulders.

"Whatever you might feel, honesty between the spouses will remain an important issue as long as civil society exists," insisted Divya.

"What you say is true, but it's funny that people should view faithfulness as the sole virtue upon which a married relationship should hinge," Shivani argued with little conviction.

For a moment, they stopped as the train passed through the station. The engine let out a loud whistle. Both peeped into the dark and tried to read the station's name, but in vain. The night like that did strange things to the people. It aroused awe in some, melancholy in some, and romance in others. But they sought something different.

Divya stood up, opened the bag and pulled out a steel thermos flask. She asked Shivani, uncorking it, "Would you care for some coffee?

"Why didn't you give it earlier?"

"Oh, it slipped out of my mind then. I recollected when I saw the station."

"Thanks. Coffee is my weakness. I can drink it anytime of the day or night. In fact, if somebody wakes me up in the middle of the night and offers it, I won't refuse." Shivani's face lit up.

"I hope it's hot. The company advertises that their flasks keep drinks hot or cold for up to twenty-four hours. Let's check their claim," Divya said, pouring coffee into two glasses.

"Wow! It's really hot. Thanks." Shivani was ecstatic.

They sipped coffee at leisure, exchanging smiles in between. Shivani had a passion for coffee and often had it with her husband on the lawn and the balcony, watching the sun set behind the hills on the horizon. Those moments were precious for her, as he discussed with her the theme, characters and plot of his novel. She listened to him with rapt attention and gave her suggestions, which he sometimes included. He valued her ideas and admired her intelligence.

"Thinking about hubby?" Divya asked.

"Yeah, you're right. Coffee reminds me of him. He discusses his book with me over a cup of coffee."

"Lucky girl. At least your man has time to drink coffee with you. Mine doesn't sit with me even for a few minutes. I often eat alone. I can't recall when we had our last dinner together. Business is his first love, and I get the last priority."

"You're being harsh to him. There are no businessmen in my family, but I empathise with them. After all, running a business requires a lot of time and hard work."

"You're right, but earning money is not everything in life. He ought to give time to me. I don't know how to spend time alone in a large bungalow."

"Maybe you should join the kitty parties or spend time in social activities about which we read in the newspapers and magazines."

"I wish I could, but I'm not like them. My mindset is different because I grew up in a small place. I don't like parties and social work. I find them a big sham."

"But the media and the peer attention are so exciting."

"I find it boring; in fact, vulgar and farcical."

Their discussion was getting serious, so Shivani changed the topic. "What about your kids? Where are they?"

"We are yet to start a family. Perhaps we will plan within a few years." Divya's voice deepened with sadness. Though she wanted a child, her husband showed no interest. He avoided the issue for the reasons best known to him.

"It's good to have kids. They give a nice company when husband is away."

"Yeah, but I can't produce them alone. I need his help." Divya winked, bringing a smile to Shivani's face.

"Isn't it strange that the woman who carries the child in her womb has no say in the matter when and how many children she should have? It's always the man who has the last say," Shivani said with a deep sigh.

"Yeah, it's a man's world, whether we like it or don't. So, next time when God asks you for your choice, ask Him to make you a man," Divya teased.

"No, I didn't mean that. I'm better off as a woman," Shivani shot back.

Loud rattle of the bogey wheels and the shrill engine whistles interrupted their talks. Disruption had become a routine. When the train crossed the station or the bridge, it made loud noises in whose din it was impossible for them to talk.

"What's the time?" Shivani asked.

"11 p.m.," said Divya, "I hope I'm not keeping you awake. You can go to sleep. I'll take some more time."

"No. I'm not sleepy," Shivani smiled.

"My mother would be waiting for me," Divya said, wiping her face with her hands. "She is alone at home. I'm looking forward to spending some time with her."

"Why? Where's your father?"

"He lives in Mumbai. He left my mother a decade ago."

"Oh, I'm so sorry."

"It's all right. I've forgotten him long back."

"What led to their break-up?" Shivani asked. "I hope I'm not being too nosy."

"No," Divya replied. "I was twelve when I learnt about it. I was in the hostel then. My mother told me they had filed for divorce and soon would get separated. Since father was not keen to take me with him, the onus of raising me up fell upon my mother."

"It's so tragic."

"Yeah, but when I read about thousands of orphan girls, I forget my struggle. At least I got my mother to take care of me."

"That's the spirit. I like your philosophy of life," Shivani tried to cheer her companion up.

"What philosophy, yar? I just keep a positive attitude." Divya smiled.

Shivani sighed when Divya became herself again. She was thankful to God for giving her a great childhood with loving parents, though she was the third child after two sons.

"I can understand how hard it would have been for you."

"It's so sweet of you."

"We get one life and we should enjoy it to the fullest. I hope your hubby spends quality time with you in the future." Shivani gave her an endearing smile.

"I can't complain about my situation. I'm to blame for it." Divya's past shadowed the glow on her face.

"You shouldn't say that."

"Perhaps you don't know. There was someone who loved me so much and cared for me until I dumped him because of my stupidity."

"Is this your second marriage?"

"Hmm."

Shivani waited with bated breath. Divya peeped into the cold dark outside and said. "It happened six years ago. After my post-graduation, I worked in the Imperial Hotel in Nainital as a receptionist. The job was to tide over the financial crisis my mother faced. She'd no bank balance or property, except for a modest house in Ranikhet. Though some people advised her to ask for maintenance from my father and if he refused, then file a case against him, my mother refused. She was too proud to ask him for alimony. My mother would have preferred to die than beg for money from the man who had dumped her for a younger woman. I respected her decision then. In fact, I respect it more now.

"Neither did I meet my father, nor asked him for any monetary help. I didn't want to see his face. It's a different matter that he contacted none of us. Our lives were better without him. My mother shifted to Nainital, where we rented a house. After about a year, I met a man in the hotel. He was there for a seminar on wildlife organised by the World Wildlife Fund (WWF). Later, I gathered he was an important speaker in the seminar because of the extensive research he'd done on the subject.

"Ours was a chance meeting. One day when I was at the reception, a bearded man wearing kurta pyjama walked to the counter and asked me about a foreign delegate. I smiled at his appearance and wondered what that rustic man was doing in a three-star hotel. His sharp eyes caught me smiling, but he said nothing. Perhaps he was in a hurry. In the evening, I found an envelope with my name at the reception. Curious, I read it."

Dear Divya,

The world is not what our eyes see. The truth remains hidden until someone discovers it. Few people have the time and courage to do that. The silent majority lives a life based on false beliefs.

Yours,

Rustic

That note stung me like a bee. For the next few days, I felt ashamed. The man had read my eyes and interpreted my smile correctly. I got attracted to him. After a while, we began dating and a few months later; we got married. He was a writer, but I considered him an explorer. Before writing on any subject, he visited the places, met with the people and collected the facts. He was obsessed with the details, to the point of being insane. I hope your hubby is a normal guy?" Divya looked at Shivani in the dim light and said.

"My man is too lazy to dig out the details. He is just a writer. I think the similarities end there," Shivani said nonchalantly.

"What does he write about?" Divya asked, to clarify a few of her concerns.

"He writes fiction for which he doesn't need much research. Divya, you were telling me about your first hubby," Shivani reminded her.

"Yeah, I told you how we met and dated. He'd a soft corner for the poor. When we walked together, he'd stop and ask people on the street how they earned their livelihood. Often he'd give them money and move ahead. What surprised me the most was that he needed money to build the house, but that didn't deter him from helping the needy.

One day, he received a huge royalty for his book. With that, he purchased an old bungalow on the hillock in Nainital, where he shifted with a box full of old clothes, an old typewriter and some books. I helped him in setting up the new house. To my utter surprise and delight, he proposed to me. I accepted and the following month we got married in a simple ceremony. My life was blissful for about a year. Life with him in a beautiful hill station was a dream fulfilled. On the weekends, we went trekking in the mountains and spent nights in abandoned gaddi huts. Our honeymoon lasted a year." Divya took a breather.

The word "honeymoon" made Shivani blush. Unable to control herself, she asked, "If you don't mind, may I ask you something personal?"

"Yeah."

"How was it with him? I mean…" Shivani couldn't hide her awkwardness.

"You mean physically." Divya waited for a moment and then said with a grin, "Yeah, he was good, nothing out of the world but passionate and frequent. We lived a happy life but were often short of money, about which he never complained. But I always felt the pinch. I wanted to buy better things for us, but he seemed least interested. His life revolved around his books. When he worked on a manuscript, he forgot everything—eating, drinking, shaving, bathing or talking. When I whined, he urged me to go for a walk around the lake and leave him alone.

"During an evening walk, I met with a handsome guy. Seeing a woman alone on the bench, he approached me. He was dashing and confident young man. He introduced himself and asked me for coffee. Though I was hesitant to go with a stranger, his courteous behaviour bowled me over. Then something strange happened inside me. I developed feelings for him. We met several times. Those days were trying times for me, both mentally and physically, as my husband was busy and gave me little time. His neglect willy-nilly pushed me into the waiting arms of another man. We overstepped the boundary of our friendship on the last night of his stay. He promised to marry me after I divorced my husband. The man gave me dreams, real big dreams of a luxurious life. He'd a palatial house in Delhi with a battery of servants and earned loads of money.

"His wealth and physical prowess were too tempting for me to leave. So I planned to leave my poor husband, who had no time for my emotional or physical needs. And I worked towards achieving my goal. In a couple of months, my persistent nagging and howling made his life hell. To my delight, one day he suggested that if I wasn't happy with him, it was better to separate and end the bitterness that was destroying us. With a smile, he signed the divorce papers. We separated amicably. Next day I resigned from my job and moved to Delhi. I married my new husband in a grand ceremony.

"I couldn't believe my luck of marrying a prince and living a fairy-tale life about which the girls read only in the story books. We went for our honeymoon to Switzerland. After that, I went with him on many foreign trips. Suddenly, my world that I'd built with loyalty, honesty and hard work fell apart when I discovered my husband was sleeping with not one but many girls. I realise how important it is to have a man devoted to you and you alone, in mind and body. Despite his shortcomings, my first husband was an honest man and valued loyalty high in marriage. Having burnt my fingers, I repent now that I left him, hankering for a wealthy lifestyle. What my first husband gave me, I'd never get that in my life. I remember him running to me and sharing his first thoughts about his new book. I'd listen to him and give him my stupid suggestions that he sometimes found useful. He respected me more for my intelligence than body. My present husband treats me like a sex doll to satisfy himself when he's home."

Divya wiped her moist eyes. The story moved Shivani, who waited for her to regain her calm before clarifying a doubt, "If you're in a terrible marriage, why don't you leave him?"

"It's not that easy. How long can I hunt for Mr. Right? What's the guarantee the next man would be good? To be candid, I'm tired and have no heart for experimenting all my life. Continuing in the present relationship is my atonement for hurting a noble man. Good or bad, for me life would go on like this." Divya sank in the sea of sadness.

"Suppose your first husband forgives you and asks you to come back? Would you go back to him?" Shivani's abrupt and strange question pulled Divya out of her melancholy.

"God can't be so generous again after watching me botch it up the first time," Divya said with a forced smile. "Sorry, I bothered you with my sob story. It seems you're missing your hubby."

"Yeah." Shivani sighed. "I wonder how he can be so lazy sometimes. When I'm not at home, he'd make a mess of the house. Used plates and cups would lie all around. More clothes would be out of the cupboard than in it. The sheets and pillows would lay everywhere; in the drawing-room, bedroom and study. But he doesn't behave that way when I'm with him. He clears the mess before I enter the house. I can imagine him cleaning the house, replacing the clothes and books in the cupboards and shelves. Before I reach home, the bed would have fresh sheets and pillow covers. The house would be spick and span. He'd stay awake tonight in my wait and greet me with red eyes in the morning. Though clumsy, he is cute and helps me find happiness in small things. I love my man and would never leave him," Shivani said, but felt foolish that it could hurt Divya.

"How stupid of me? You're telling me about the man whose name I'm yet to know," Divya said.

"Abhi…"

"Abhinav," Divya prompted.

"No. Abhishek," said Shivani. Both let out a muted sigh.

"I wish you both many, many years of togetherness," Divya said and then looked at her watch. "Oh God! It's past midnight. We should catch some sleep, otherwise your hubby will blame me for keeping his sweetheart awake throughout the night."

She looked at Shivani and winked. When Divya went out, Shivani took out a piece of paper, scribbled a note, and pushed it into the inner pocket of Divya's handbag.

"Aren't you going to the washroom?" Divya asked, entering the coupe.

"Yeah."

After sometime they switched off the night lamp and fell asleep. Next morning they awoke when the train stopped at Kathgodam. They got down and looked around for the coolie.

"Thanks for the delightful company. Keep in touch." Divya hugged Shivani.

"Sure, give my love to auntie. Drop in at my place when you visit Nainital," Shivani said, handing her address.

Divya shoved it in her bag. Then they exchanged smiles, shook hands, and parted.

In the evening at Ranikhet, Divya, while searching for the suitcase key, emptied her handbag on the bed. A piece of paper startled her. She opened it and read:

Dear Divya,

It would shock you that the man you had left some years ago is with me. I'm married to him, though he has changed a lot. After you moved away from him, he has lost much of his originality. You have lost a good husband, and the world has lost a talented writer. What I have is a simple and good human being. You may rest assured that I'll take good care of him as you would wish me to.

Shivani.

Divya read the note again and again, tears streaming down her eyes. Then she prayed for both Abhinav and Shivani.

Short Story by Priyanka Joshi More

Visit Me Every Summer

"How can you not like the summers?" Geetika, my friend asked me.

"I just don't." I shrugged my shoulders.

I disliked the heat, the sun on my skin, turning red and burning. I detested the warm breeze, sweating so much that I felt like a melting ice cube. I never liked the sun even as a kid. I hated outdoor sports activities also but still had to do them. After school playtime was more fun in the evenings when the sun was setting.

"What did you do during vacations?" she asked.

"Visited my grandparents and my parents' friends. It was a fixed pattern every year for as long as I can recall."

My parents decided to travel as it was the only time we could meet the family, or better, "they" could meet their families. Schools and colleges being closed, made it practical for travelling, although in the scorching heat.

"How did you manage in the heat?" she asked, confused. I gave her a closed-mouth smile.

I do not complain about summer vacations because I did enjoy them. For all that, I do remember being irritated by the heat, suffering from rashes and prickly heat every year. My grandmothers diverted my attention to other things, as a kid, one easily does get diverted also.

"The only things I liked about summer and still do are, the yummy seasonal fruits, especially mangoes and the bright flowers blooming on the trees, especially the *gulmohars*."

"Really? Are you sure that's all?"

I chuckled at her amazement. "Yeah well, I liked some other things also such as that we travelled to meet the folks and friends and NO school!"

She rubbed her hands with her palms to warm herself as she was probably feeling cold under the air-condition, which I ran at full speed as I felt hot. Outside it was a blazing 42 C, a usual summer day in India. She had come over to spend a day with me before she left for her hometown, the following day. Our exams had finished a day before and vacations had begun. We had completed our final year of college and I too was to visit with my parents the next week.

"So will you be going this summer to visit your grandparents?"

"Yes, I might, depends on my parents."

"What about Ishan?"

"What about him?"

"Won't you be visiting him also?"

"Maybe...come let's eat." I changed the topic.

***

Each year, every summer, Ishan Goyal was the most awaited part of my summer vacation since childhood. We grew up together as he was the son of my parents' friends and we would visit them every summer, spending an entire week there. As kids we were friends who played together, ate together and slept together. There were times when my parents left me there for days. I was pampered, spoiled and loved spending my time there. The days would pass away playing, watching TV and so on, some best memories of my childhood.

As the years passed, he got busier with a variety of extra-curricular summer activities which kept him busy, but still, whenever possible he would join me in whatever activity I was up to. During the summer vacation when puberty had hit, things changed drastically, as we were no longer allowed to share a bed. Life was suddenly all about future goals and careers, summer courses, extra classes and other activities. We did meet and talk about things whenever the time permitted. It was the only time I got with him.

It was the next year, two years back from now, that a substantial change came into effect. That year, when I was in the first year of college, after exams I went to visit my parents and we visited Ishan's parents. I still remember, when we reached, he wasn't home and we had breakfast. After that, I decided to freshen up and when I returned from my bath, a familiar face smiled at me. It was Ishan, but he looked different as he had a growth spurt and facial hair.

"Hi," he said as he waved and smiled. Hearing him I realised his voice had also changed.

"Hey," is all I could reply being mentally occupied noticing the changes in him.

We exchanged formal pleasantries. The entire day, I did not meet or talk to him. As there was a wedding, everyone was caught up in it. That evening, after dinner I decided to step outside on the terrace for some fresh air. I kept the main door open and the mosquito net door shut but unlocked so that it was noticeable that I was there before someone locked it. Thinking about a variety of things while watching the city lights and planes flying above, since it was close to the airport, my thoughts were broken when I heard the door open.

"Who's here?" a voice asked. A strange voice but not completely unknown.

"It's me," I replied to Ishan.

"What are you doing out here? That too alone?" he confronted.

"Just came to get some fresh air."

"Come inside, it is not safe, also there are mosquitoes that will bite you, come on, come inside," he instructed.

For a moment, I felt as if Ishan had changed, he was no longer the friendly fun-loving guy – the friend I loved to hang out with. He was so grown up, telling me what to do and not to do, like he was my guardian and responsible for me. I walked inside while he locked the door.

"Don't go on the terrace in the dark, it is not safe for you and the house. Thefts have become common nowadays here. Everyone has been asking for you downstairs, you had not mentioned to anyone where you were," he said in a stern tone still facing the door. I stood watching him from behind.

Even though I did feel like saying sorry, I did not. His tone irked me, he was not my parent or guardian but he acted like it. Before he could turn, I left.

The next day, the women went shopping and I too had to tag along spending all day visiting various malls and markets. That evening after we reached home, I was tired. I went to the room and lay down, while everyone was having tea downstairs when there was a knock on the door. I opened my eyes when Ishan opened the door, so I sat up.

"Sorry to bother you, I needed some stuff…" he paused, looking at me. Then he asked, "You okay? You look tired."

I nodded. "I'm fine."

"Shopping, huh?" he asked teasingly.

I nodded again; I was too worn out to reply. He stood there leaning on the chest of drawers.

"Did you buy something for yourself?" he asked again. It was evident he wanted to talk but I couldn't. I shook my head. He probably got the signal, he picked up some stuff from his study table and walked out, before closing the door, he said, "Take rest."

I lay down and shut my eyes and soon fell asleep. As it was already evening, and one should not sleep at odd hours; it was probably an hour later when the door knocked again and someone opened it. I was too tired to open my eyes and see.

"It's late, you should get up." It was Ishan again.

He switched on the lights and the darkroom became brightly lit. I sat up, rubbing my eyes.

"How long have I been asleep?"

"Around two hours. The servant had brought you juice and snacks but I told him not to disturb you, as you were resting."

"Where is everyone?"

"They are downstairs, busy with something, I am not sure as I was working in the next room all this while."

I got up to go to the washroom and when I returned, I noticed a tray with a glass of juice, a glass of water and some sandwiches on the side table while he sat on the couch, near the bed.

"You should have it," he signalled at the contents of the tray.

I sat on the bed and drank water. Then I sipped the juice.

"Sandwich?"

I took one to be polite although I wasn't that hungry. I ate in silence. While eating, I noticed his eyes, he had thick black lashes like a natural mascara applied. I had seen these eyes multiple times, but I noticed them only today. He was avoiding eye contact as I was eating and when I realised I was staring into his, seemed quite rude, I too looked the other way.

"So how are things with you?" he asked after I wiped my mouth with the paper napkin.

I smiled. I began telling him about my college, my friends, and the city. He listened with interest. Time flew by talking until we were called for dinner. It felt like the olden days again. After dinner, his mother suggested we go out for ice cream – just like the old days. There was a dessert place near his house, which had good ice cream, cakes, pastries and cookies – all things yum. I had a sweet tooth then and now. I was super-excited. We went to the dessert place, everyone ordered what they wanted and after much thinking, I decided to go with Choco-chip ice cream, which was my all-time choice there. Meanwhile, they all patiently waited for me to finalise.

"Are you sure that's what you want? After spending so much time pondering what to have, you decide to go for the same flavour again?" he asked me jokingly.

He was waiting so he could pay at the counter. I nodded. Soon, our orders arrived, the parents were sitting outside on the patio, while we were sitting inside. The smell of cookies made me hungry. He brought a tray with our orders, and the three of us sat at one table, Ishan, his younger brother and me.

"God, this place still has the most delicious ice cream," I remarked as I had the first spoon. He smiled.

"You want to taste mine?" he offered.

I hesitated for a moment, but this was not the first time we ate from the same plate or bowl, in fact, quite frequently as kids, so I took a small bite of what looked like chocolate but tasted different.

"It's called death by chocolate," he stated before I could ask.

"It's different."

"That's why I ordered it," he replied. I offered him mine, and he took a tiny bit on his spoon, probably just to be polite. He told me about the time he visited another city some time back for an internship when went to an ice-cream shop, having the same flavour for the first time there and since then became a fan of it. He also described how the flavour got its name. I kept listening and eating quietly, nodding in between. I was happy he was excited to share something with me; recently, I missed that.

The next morning was super busy as it was the wedding day. Ishan left early with his mother to the venue while we went a little later. When we reached the venue, he did acknowledge my presence with a smile. I hoped Ishan would complement me but he hardly noticed. I stayed close to my parents as I was not comfortable around strangers. While I was at the buffet, choosing the dishes, Ishan emerged from behind and suggested to me a few dishes I must try, which he was certain I would enjoy. I accepted his suggestion and went for the dishes. Indeed, he was right, I did love them.

That night I returned home early along with my parents while he and his family returned quite late. I had to pack my bags as I was to leave the day after. We had come for the wedding and now that was over. My parents went to bed but I was up packing. I heard the car drive into the gate. Next, I heard footsteps and hushed voices. I opened the door when the voices seemed pretty close. It was Ishan and his mother.

"You're still awake *beta*?" she asked me.

"Yes, I was not sleepy so I decided to complete some packing."

"Okay," she whispered. She left for her room and Ishan turned to look at me.

"Done with packing?" he asked.

"Yes, almost. How was the wedding?"

"You did see almost all of it, except the *bidaai* (the ceremony in which the bride departs the parents' home). Yes, it happened."

I nodded.

"Okay then, good night."

I nodded again. I did not understand why I had changed. I was a chirpy, loud and talkative person, but in front of Ishan, I became a completely different person altogether. I nodded to more than half of his statements and questions. Why was I behaving like that?

He left to go to the room and I shut the door to mine. For the next two days, he and I barely got the time to interact. He was in his room all day and stepped out only for lunch and dinner. That time we ate in silence, except for things like, "shall I pass this to you?" or "please pass me that." I wanted to talk to him, but it was no use. I left the next day with an early morning flight, hoping to meet him next year. Every single time each year, from the day before I was to leave, he became distant, did not talk properly and usually, I left at odd hours, which meant he would either be asleep or out. He was never there to see me off.

The next year, once again after exams my parents informed me that they had made travel plans and we were to stay over at Ishan's place for approximately a week. My heart jumped with joy on hearing it, but I also felt nervous. The day arrived when I was to reach his place. Mother had informed me that Ishan now had a job. When we reached there, his parents welcomed us warmly as always and obviously, as always, he was not around. Even his younger brother who was also my playmate as a child was now busy with his friends and classes. Like always, I was put up in Ishan's room, while he had shifted to the next room, which was now transformed into his study/TV room. There was a couch that turned into a bed, so either he could sleep on it or he could share his brother's bed. The house had been renovated so it seemed different yet nice. That evening, I went to the market as my friends had given me a list of things they wanted and when I returned home, mother and aunty called me for dinner. I told them first I would go to my room to keep my bags, freshen up and then join them. As I climbed the stairs, Ishan appeared at the top of the staircase.

"I thought I heard your voice," he said once again with a smile.

"Hey Ishan, how are you?"

As I climbed up the stairs my eyes gazed at him, he was so handsome compared to last time. He now had stubble, he was taller and slightly muscular. He was not the boy I played with, he was now, a young handsome man.

"Good, and you?" he replied when I reached the top.

"All good." I smiled back.

"Coming for dinner?"

"Yes, I'll be down soon, go ahead."

He nodded and climbed down the stairs. I watched him without realising that I was. Just then, I remembered that I had to place the bags in the room, so I did that, washed my hands and face, and then went down for dinner. That night, while I was in my room, I heard footsteps but I did not open the door. Soon there was a knock on my door. As I opened it, Ishan said, "Your lights were on, so I decided to check if you're awake."

"Yeah, I was just reading, you want to come in?"

He entered.

"So, what are you reading?"

"A novel my friend suggested to me by an Indian author."

"What is it about?"

"Romance. Tell me what's up with you?."

He sat on the chair and talked about his job for nearly an hour.

"Don't you have to get up early for work?" I asked him.

"Yes, I better get going. Good night."

"Good night."

He left the room and I closed the door. Talking to Ishan felt so calming. That night I slept smiling to myself. Since my last visit, I had been thinking about Ishan more often than usual. The next day, when I woke up as there was a knock on the door, he was getting ready to go to work and needed something from his room. I sat up on the bed and called out, "Come in."

He entered the room, apologising for waking me.

"It's alright."

He collected some papers. "See you later," he said as he rushed out.

"Have a good day." I smiled at him.

That evening, as Ishan had not returned home, I was watching TV with his brother in the TV room after dinner. His brother left to attend a call. I was alone when unexpectedly, the door opened, and Ishan walked in. I was startled.

"Sorry, I didn't mean to startle you." He placed his bag on the table and loosened his tie.

"No, it's fine." I got up to leave.

"Where are you going?" he asked, opening his sleeve buttons and pulling his sleeves up. "I'll go to my room; you must need your room."

"Don't be silly, you can watch TV, I have to eat dinner anyway, it's not like I have to sleep."

He signalled me to remain seated and went to the washroom. Soon he returned while the servant brought his dinner served on a plate along with a jug of water and an empty glass. The servant placed the tray on the table and left. As Ishan was busy wiping his hands and face, I decided to help. I turned over the lid that covered his dinner, placed the plate on the table, filled the glass with water from the jug and placed it next to the plate also. Even I was unaware of why I was doing that. He noticed it too.

"You don't have to do all that."

"Just trying to help, you're back so late so I thought you might be hungry."

I looked away feeling shy, unable to face him, for what I had done unknowingly, so I could not see his reaction. I went back to staring at the TV. This was new, I thought. I felt shy in front of Ishan. But why?

He sat down on the adjoining sofa to eat. "What are you watching?" he asked, eyes focused on the screen.

I held out the remote in front of him, another action I did unknowingly. He turned to look at me, confused.

"I only asked what you were watching, I didn't ask for the remote."

I placed the remote on the table. "Sorry."

He gaped at me but turned back to his food. He ate in silence, probably confused at my behaviour while my thoughts were pretty loud. How could I be so stupid? What have I done?

"I think I should leave, you must want to sleep," I said as he ate his last bite.

"No, stay for a while, if you feel like it."

I complied. We sat there for a few minutes when something funny on TV made us crack up in laughter. We laughed for a long time, thinking about it over and over, till my stomach hurt and my eyes watered. It led us to talk about childhood memories, how we watched cartoons, built forts of sofa cushions, funny moments, places we visited together, stuff we ate together; memories brought smiles, some he recalled and other things I reminded him.

"Good night, it's very late now," I said looking at the clock. He nodded. I walked out of the room, shutting the door behind and walked over to my room. It felt nice that he too remembered our memories. It made me forget about the weird things I had done that same night.

The next morning when I woke up, I came to know he had already left for work. When he returned early in the evening, he seemed pretty tired and went for a nap, likely as he slept late that night and left early in the morning. At dinner, he did join us but he did not talk to me. I was heading towards my room when he called me from behind and asked if I would sit with him for a while. I agreed. I waited for him in my room when thirty minutes later there was a knock on my door, it was him. He asked me to come to the TV room, and I followed.

"What do you want to talk about?" I asked him as I sat on the sofa and he closed the door.

"Nothing special, just old memories," he said in a calm voice.

I was surprised. I smiled. "Sure."

We reminisced about the old days, we went swimming classes together and once my eyes were burning due to the chemicals in the pool, I cried the entire time even after returning home. My mother was not there, so his parents took care of me. Ishan sat beside me the entire time trying to pacify me; when there was something I fought with my mother about and sat in a corner upset, he would come and lift my mood; or when he was sad, I went to talk to him about it and he was always keen to know about what I was doing, where I was and in my stuff.

"Such good days," I said, sighing loudly. He looked at me with a grin.

"It's late again, we should sleep."

The clock had struck midnight. I got up to leave.

"You know, except for my cousins, you are the only girl I am comfortable with," he stated.

I was not surprised. Somehow, I knew he was telling the truth. I nodded. I walked out of the room and he got up to close the door. Before I entered my room and he would close his door, I turned around and said, "You know, you are my only childhood friend, not from school."

He smiled. I entered my room and whispered, "good night." He nodded and shut his door. That night I could not sleep, I kept tossing in bed thinking about

Ishan. He was unlike the other guys I knew as friends from college. He was shy, quiet and not very social, I had realised that by now.

The next morning, he was having breakfast when I went down for breakfast. He left while I was eating. That evening, when he returned, I asked him if we could talk for a while, but he declined, saying he had work.

"If I complete my work soon, I will call you." He assured me.

I went to my room, waiting for him to come, but he never did. By 11 p.m, his room lights were out. I felt hurt. All these days, when he wanted to, he talked to me, staying up till midnight, but today when I wanted to, he denied and slept early too. I was annoyed at his behaviour. The next morning, he was out before I woke up. I explained to myself that he probably had to leave early so he slept early. That evening, I felt he would come and apologise, but he did not. He did not even join us for dinner. His mother informed us that he had some work, so he will eat in his room. When I went up to my room, his lights were on but as I opened the door to my room, the lights were out. He probably had not eaten either. I felt he was avoiding me, so I decided to distance myself too. The next evening, when he returned, I stayed occupied with other things on purpose. I sat till midnight talking with mother and aunty. When I went to my room, his lights were off, but as I entered my room, his door opened.

"You're up till so late, I…"

"I was with my mother and your mother," I interrupted him mid-sentence.

"Okay."

"You should go to sleep, these days you sleep early," I said sarcastically. He did not reply. I entered the room and closed the door, while he stood watching. I did not like the way I behaved. As kids, although we fought, it was for toys or who is better at school, but this was something unusual. My brusque remark at him, him ignoring me, what had happened to us? I began to sob silently.

The next morning, I decided not to leave bed soon as it was the weekend and I knew Ishan would be home. I felt guilty to face him. Mother came to check on me thinking I was not up yet, but when she saw me awake, she questioned me why I had not joined for breakfast. I lied to her, I was feeling low. She said she would have breakfast sent to my room. I stayed there all day, but I could not stay there forever. I had to come out at some point so I decided to go down for lunch. When I reached, everyone was there except Ishan. I came to know that he went out with his friends and will return late. Here I was sad and upset, there he was least bothered. That night, I was in my room reading, when I heard Ishan's door opening. I decided to stay put, as I had nothing to say to him, it was for the best that we did not face each other. There was a knock on my door a while later but I switched off the lights, and the knocking stopped. I felt upset and annoyed at the same time.

As I had to leave the day after and I was aware that Ishan would distance himself, I decided to make it easy for him and on me, by not stepping out of the room that often. I asked my food to be sent to the room. That night I turned off the lights early too. The next day was Monday. I woke up and went down for breakfast. Mother asked me if packing was complete to which I told her it was. We had to catch an early hour flight, so we planned to have an early dinner. At dinner, while we were eating, Ishan's mother acknowledged his arrival. He was home. As a natural instinct, I turned to look at him. He was handing his lunch box to the servant when our eyes met. I looked away. Aunty went up to him, explaining to him why we were having an early dinner. He spoke with her and then left to go to his room. After dinner, I sat with the parents as they were talking. My mind was occupied with Ishan, but I did not wish to face him as I knew he would not talk properly and that would hurt me more. The servant informed Aunty that Ishan called his dinner upstairs to his room. Later, I went to my room when I saw Ishan standing at his door.

"Do you have a moment?"

"I think I should sleep; I have to get up early," I responded coldly.

"Please, it won't take long," he requested.

"Why? When I want to talk to you, you go away, so why should I?" I snapped at him.

"Look I am sorry, I know you're upset with me, all I wanted to say was…"

"Enough, Ishan! I am tired of behaving as per your convenience, when you want to talk, I should come and talk, when you want to ignore me, I should act as if nothing happened." My voice was rising so I toned it down so no one heard. "And when I have to leave, two days prior to my departure, you behave as if I don't exist!"

I walked into the room, so no one could hear anything, while he stood at the door.

"I've had enough. For you, I am probably just your parents' friend's daughter who visits every summer, but for me, you were always special, my childhood friend. I long to talk to you and spend time with you, but you don't feel any of that for me. I have understood it."

He remained silent.

Tears rolled out my eyes. "You never knew how special you are to me, so close to my heart that I have..." I stopped. What was I saying? What was I about to say? I froze. I hadn't realised it myself till now. I did not look at him so I couldn't see his reaction. We stood still and silent for a while, till he shut the door to my room.

I sat on the bed rewinding what just happened. Was this true? Had I fallen in love? With Ishan? What must he be thinking? So many questions and no answers, it was painful. I tried to sleep but could not. It was in the deep of the night, that I probably dozed off. The alarm had been set for 5 a.m. I realised I had been asleep when the alarm woke me. I sat up, thinking about Ishan and the previous night when I noticed what looked like a small bag on the bedside table. I reached for it and looked inside. It was an expensive perfume, an international brand.

There was a note inside that read:

Dear Saumya,

I know we have not been able to talk much recently, I am sorry. This is one of the gifts I had promised you when we were kids, as a token of our special bond. Hope you like it. Take care,

Ishan.

PS: I will miss you.

My eyes welled up. He remembered. It was this time when we went shopping as young teenagers and I was fascinated by one brand of perfume which had a lovely fragrance. I asked Mother to buy it for me but she refused. I was upset with her when he consoled me by saying, "Don't worry, when I get a job, I will buy it for you." I smiled. Later I forgot all about it. But he remembered. I could not control my joy, so I quickly went to his room, but then before I knocked on his door, I stopped thinking he must be asleep and I turned to go back.

I went to my room and quickly got a pen and paper and wrote a note:

Dear Ishan,

Thank you so much for the lovely gift. I was so overjoyed to know that you remembered. I am sorry for my behaviour last night. I should not have spoken so rudely to you; we are friends first and that's important to me. You are and will always remain special.

But something I could not say last night, I want to say now. It is also true that I have fallen in love with you. When and how even I don't know. I know you don't love me, and no force either. But I just wanted to convey my feelings to you. Please don't get mad at me. I don't want to ruin our friendship.

Friends first always,

Saumya.

I left the note on his table. I got dressed and went down to leave for the airport. During the flight, I kept wondering if he'd seen the letter and how he might have reacted. Would he have been angry, sad or unaffected? What if someone else found the letter before him? That was the last I heard from Ishan. Some of my close friends including Geetika knew about us.

***

After Geetika left, my phone rang. It was Mother. She informed me that Grandmother was unwell so they were leaving to visit her, and as my tickets were already booked, they changed the destination, so now I had to stay with Ishan's parents for a week. My heart skipped a beat. How would I face Ishan now?

The day arrived when I had to travel and my flight landed twenty minutes late. When I walked out from the arrival, I decided to wait for my network to connect on roaming so I could call a cab. Just then, I was tapped on the shoulder. I turned around to see who it was and to my surprise, it was Ishan and his brother.

"What are you guys doing here?"

"We came to pick you," his brother replied. Ishan only smiled and took my bag.

"How was your flight?"

"Good. But why did you take the trouble? I would've taken a cab."

"Mom wanted *bhaiya* to pick you up since you were coming alone, and I tagged along."

I thanked Aunty silently. I was over delighted to see them, especially Ishan there. We reached home and I was put up in the guest room this time as my parents were not with me, who usually got that room. I was uncertain on how to talk to Ishan, generally and about the letter. We did not speak much. Uncle and Aunty were busy asking me about Grandmother, while Ishan kept listening silently. After dinner I went to my room, as I was closing the door to my room, he was climbing the stairs, we looked at each other and smiled. He wished me goodnight and so did I. The next evening, his parents had to attend a function of some of their friends. Ishan and his brother were to accompany them. Aunty was uncertain to leave me alone, but I reassured her that I will be fine. Later Ishan called from work that he won't be coming due to work. They left around 8 p.m, and by 8:30 p.m Ishan was home.

"I thought you were going to be late?" I asked, surprised that he reached so soon. He did not react, handing his lunchbox to the servant, ordering him to serve dinner. He turned to me.

"You ate?"

"Not yet."

He ordered the servant to place our dinner on the table. He went up the stairs to his room, probably to change. I stood there staring at him. He arrived later, while I helped the servant serve dinner and took his seat.

"Come eat." I nodded.

"How was work?" I asked.

We ate, talking about his work and other things in general. After dinner was over, he went to wash his hands while I helped the servant pick up the dishes. He emerged from behind and asked, "Do you want to go for ice cream?" I shook my head. "I want to talk to you."

I was sure now he was going to talk about the letter. I looked at him.

"In my room, then?" he confirmed. I nodded. He left to go upstairs. I took a while winding up and then went to his room.

I knocked on his door. "Come in," he said so I opened the door. He was watching TV.

"Sit." I obeyed.

"Saumya, I want to talk about last summer."

We looked at each other.

"I don't know where to start?" he said nervously.

"Ishan, let's just forget what happened. It was last year, it's passed."

"Is it that easy for you to let go?"

"I don't know what you are talking about?"

"I am talking about the letter you left for me on my table, Saumya." I looked at him nervously.

"About that, I …" I began talking when he interrupted me.

"Do you have any idea how I felt when you tried to imply that I did not care about you? Or that you were not special to me? Saumya, I was busy, but that doesn't mean I never cared," he said in an irritated voice.

"Ishan…" I began to talk, but he interrupted me again.

"No, you listen to me first, as kids we played together but even then, whenever you were to leave, I would get sad; I worried about you, at times I might have been strict but that was because I cared; I was busy in making a career so I could become financially independent..." He paused. I stared at him because each time I began talking he interrupted me so I waited for him to go on.

"Saumya, all I am saying is that you can't tell me how you feel and judge me, without hearing my side."

"Do you love me, Ishan?" I went right to the point. He turned to face me and looked me in the eyes.

"I do."

I was speechless, I had not been expecting him to say it. I could not believe what I heard.

"Wait, what?"

He nodded.

"Aren't you going to say anything?"

"I am going to my room." I rushed out from there, ran down the stairs and into my room. A moment later, there was a knock on my door.

"Saumya, open the door." But I didn't budge.

Instead of being happy and over the top, I had blanked out. He knocked again repeatedly for a number of times but when I did not open, he left. An hour later, his family arrived home but I turned off my lights so everyone would think I was asleep. I sat on the bed in the dark for hours thinking about our childhood memories till present.

The next morning, as usual, Ishan left for work and I was confined to my room. I recalled all the incidents from the last 2 years. That evening when he returned, we glanced at each other and he left for his room. He did not come down the entire evening. The next evening was the same. I could sense he was upset with me. He was the silent type who when upset cut himself off from others. So, the third evening, I decided to talk to him but he returned late after I had fallen asleep. The next day, his parents had to go out of town for a night. He couldn't go as he had office work. That day I decided to wait for him till whatever hour he returned, to talk to him. I sat on the chair waiting, but I did not realise I had dozed-off till I felt a tap on my shoulder.

"What are you doing out here?" Ishan asked angrily.

"I want to talk to you."

"It's late, go sleep," he instructed in a stern tone and began climbing the stairs.

"No. I won't. I want to talk to you." I was not going to give up today.

He stood on the stairs looking at me. "There is nothing to talk about."

"Yes, there is," I said, climbing the stairs and reaching him.

"Did I ever tell you that I had a childhood best friend I met every summer, each year till I fell in love with him. I was not sure he loved me and when he told me he did, I did not know how to react. I thought I knew him so well, but I never understood him, his feelings and his behaviour. It was my mistake for which I want to apologise. I am sorry I hurt you, Ishan, and I love you."

His expressions changed. We smiled. He raised his arms to hug and I hugged him. We had hugged many times as friends but this felt completely different. I placed my head on his chest, closed my eyes and took a deep sigh.

Poem by Indrani Chowdhury

The Manifold Colours of Summer Waves

The hell-bent heat waves of summer "roar,"

Ravaging the calm symphony of shadowy corridors,

Invading each such corner with scorching light.

It is as if it is throwing down the gauntlet,

To devour each cooling outlet,

With its hot raging tides.

The recalcitrant sun,

After jotting down the vulnerabilities of,

Humans, flowers, birds, and beasts,

Lashes out with its heat waves without cease.

The extremities of this megalomaniac,

Seems to be taking a toll on flowers,

As in the face of such heat,

They risk being withered away or of losing their lustrous glow.

And the birds and beasts,

In their relentless pursuit to get some respite from such heat,

Persistently return to their water holes.

Their ceaseless thirst,

Tease their noble endeavours,

To remain patient in the face of such a crisis.

It seems the tyrant sun never tires up,

To complete every day its victory lap,

Ending up intimidating humans.

For its beams could pierce their skin,

Sucking the much-needed energy from within.

The heat stroke, the perspiration, the obnoxious body odour,

And the prickly heats protruding from the skin with such fervour could,

Smother their zeal, setting in disorder.

On the other hand,

Another story unfolds,

In this fiercely burning land.

The local bazaar is found oozing with,

The manifold flavours of summer,

As luscious mangoes, watermelons, litchis, jackfruits,

Parade its fruit stalls,

Seducing the olfactory sense of all.

Even a seasoned buyer,

With all his bargaining power,

Could be lured to buy a little more fruit,

To savour this seasonal taste,

Without contemplating much about his financial waste.

Summer is also the time to savour the ice-cool treats.

It is the time to give a guilt-free trip to the neighbouring ice cream parlour,

And taste ice creams to beat the heat.

All fall in the vacation mode and plan soul nourishing getaways,

As summer vacation sets in.

It is a time to plan trips, to pick a hobby,

To join summer camps or to participate in community welfare gatherings.

Summer with its raging heat waves and blissful offerings,

Remain an enigma while surpassing all our expectations with its actions.

We could not and should not attempt to define,

These manifold colours of summer's revelations.

Short Story by Kuntala Bhattacharya

The Stranger at the Doorsteps

The Unusual Arrival

It was 7 PM on a Friday. Susan had just returned from the office party and after a warm shower decided to prepare a hot and strong coffee for herself.

With the water bubbling inside the coffee maker, she switched on the TV to catch on the latest news. The common faces of the BBC newsreaders appeared with the latest headlines.

The coffee was ready by then and she poured it into her favourite Italian coffee mug. The mug was very special for her, gifted by her parents on her 28th birthday this year.

She seated herself on the sofa, preparing to relax with the coffee and the thrilling news of the amazing escape from a fire, flashing on the television.

Suddenly, the front door of her house vibrated with a banging sound. Startled, Susan jumped up and stared at the door. Her heart started pounding with sudden fear.

Though her house was by the roadside, it was in a very safe locality with no reports of any unusual behaviour of miscreants.

Holding her breath, she waited for any more movement and sound. The deafening silence started to bother her. Gaining her courage, she decided to open the door and check out.

She went to the kitchen and took the knife in her hand, preparing herself for the worse. Slowly she approached the front door and peeped through the keyhole. She could not trace anyone. An eerie feeling started creeping over her.

"God, I need courage. Please be at my side. I need strength," murmured Susan to herself.

Staying alone in the apartment for almost 2 years, Susan never felt insecure. Though occasionally her parents come and visit her, she has managed to carry along with her life quite smartly.

Slowly Susan caught hold of the doorknob and turned around to open it, ensuring she didn't create a sound. The door opened and then, "Oh! My God," screamed Susan.

A man, dressed in a white shirt and blue jeans, fell near the door losing his balance in front of Susan. He seemed to have been sitting with his back placed at the door. The moment he fell and heard Susan's scream, he jumped up with a bag clasped in his hand and tried hiding inside the garden.

Susan had a special interest in gardening and had prepared a small flower bed near the front gate of her house.

Susan stared at the man, shivering in fear and looking here and there unable to guess where to flee. Spellbound and confused, Susan lost her mind for a minute. She looked outside to find out if anyone was observing them or any unusual movements. There seemed to be none.

With the knife clasped in her hand and the mobile torch beam, she started moving towards the man. As she proceeded closer, the man uttered in a vibrating tone, "Please, please, don't kill me. Please don't hurt me. I want to live please."

Susan stopped, she could not believe her ears. Something seemed to be very wrong with the man. He did not look to be normal.

Is this man a psychic? Will he attack her? Will he try to kill her?

Will she call the police? Will she call the security guard?

Multiple questions started reining through her brain.

She looked at the eyes of the man. There seemed to be innocence hidden inside along with the fear of something unknown. An inner consciousness seemed to convince her that the man needed help.

She dropped the knife from her hand and approached the man. "Don't worry, I won't harm you. Please trust me. I will help you," whispered Susan.

The man seemed to be deterred from moving. Susan could understand that he is unable to believe her. "Come here, come. Do you like to eat something? Do you want to have some coffee? Why are you afraid? Has anyone harmed you?" Susan tried to assure him.

He seemed to be in his late twenties, half shaven and with decent clothes and shoes. He lifted his head and with slow steps moved towards Susan. Susan ushered him towards the front door to get inside the house. Steadily he followed Susan and crossed the front door to enter inside.

Susan closed the door, doubting herself whether she took the correct step in welcoming a stranger inside her house.

The Mournful Childhood

Susan switched off the television.

"Please feel comfortable. Have a seat," ushered Suman.

Still quivering with fear and with slow steps, the man seated himself at the corner of the sofa. He tried to squeeze himself as much as he could in a small space, with nervousness and confusion in his eyes.

Susan seated herself at the opposite side. "What is your name? Where are you from?" asked Susan in an assuring voice.

"D…D…David," whispered the man in a trembling voice.

"Where do you stay? Where is your house? Have you lost the way to your house?" queried Susan.

"No, no, no." He started shaking his head.

Susan, a senior psychiatrist by profession, was now able to guess that David seemed to be mentally challenged. She had observed similar behaviour in many of her patients and understood the mental trauma they go through in their lives.

She put on her expert hat and decided to extract as much as the information she could from him. She understood David needed help and she felt he had either escaped from his house or had been driven out of the house.

She framed all the questions in her mind and placed it in front of David. Her first objective was to make him comfortable and remove the unknown fear residing within him. Then understand his background and the reason for his strange visit to her house.

The next two hours passed by with a lot of trials and errors. Susan was now successful in creating a story of David.

David was the sole child of his parents. His father left for heavenly abode when he was 12 years old. From then on, his mother struggled to run the household with a mentally challenged kid. She sold off her house for money and went to stay at David's grandparent's house.

David's grandparents had passed away by then. The house was mainly occupied by his father's brothers along with their families. David's grandfather owned a huge property and he had left a share to each one of his sons. David and his mother shifted with their part of share. David's uncles and their families did not entertain them as they had planned secretly to occupy their brother's share.

David's father had moved away from the house when David was born. His father knew that to bring up a mentally challenged kid, they had to shift to a place devoid of any distractions and unnecessary mental distress for him.

David and his mother had to face enormous mental trauma by his uncles' families. But his mother had no option but to continue. She had to send David to a special school and be cautious of him every moment. With meagre earnings from her job as a cook, she could not afford to rent a house.

Life was going on for both of them with a lot of struggles. To add to their worries, David's mother suddenly fell ill. The doctor diagnosed her with severe pneumonia. David was completely lost when his mother was admitted to the hospital. He never went home but sat near the hospital bed, waiting for his mother to recover. His mother's health deteriorated further and she passed away leaving David completely alone in the world.

The hospital authorities assisted him to complete the last rites. He returned to his grandparent's house without any idea of what to do. He had no one to take care of him and an unusual fear gripped him from inside.

His uncles took full advantage of David's painful situation and drove him out of the house. It was on that fatal day David had unknowingly traversed into Susan's house.

The Unusual Relation

Another set of questions was now hovering over Susan's head.

"Is it correct to provide David a shelter in my house? Will my parents like the idea? How will I handle his mental tantrums if he creates disturbance in the neighbourhood?"

It was almost 10 PM so Susan decided to finish off dinner. She escorted David to the guest room. "Be comfortable, no one will harm you here. Change into any dress you have inside your bag. You need to have some food, you seem to be starving," said Susan in a calm voice.

Susan had hired a cook one year back. The cook, a middle-aged lady, would come early in the morning every day and prepare two courses of meals: lunch and dinner.

Susan arranged the dinner table with the cutleries and served two plates. David emerged out of the guest room and stood near the dining table. He had changed himself into a house dress and kept his head bowed down in shyness.

"Please sit down and have your food. I have served dinner for you. Eat and have a nice sleep. It was a tiring day for you today. Take some rest. Tomorrow we will decide what to do next," said Susan in a soothing tone.

Nodding his head obediently, David finished off his dinner. Susan assisted him to eat properly. She then guided him to his room to sleep. Like a little kid and with fearful eyes, David went to sleep cuddling himself up at one corner of the bed.

Susan's eyes suddenly became watery at the sight of David. She felt pity for him, the struggle the poor soul must be going through with not a single person in the world beside him. Over and above David was mentally challenged who would be torn apart by miseries and traumas unless protected by someone who will take good care of him.

"Susan, it is you. Only you can save this poor soul." Susan was startled by the voice. The voice was her heart speaking out to her.

She seemed to feel a fond affection towards David. His innocence and simplicity were too precarious and if left unattended in the strange world outside would be mercilessly destroyed.

That night Susan decided to face all the odds and protect David with all her means and help him survive. She decided to treat him with all her learnings and seek expert opinions to make him suitable to stand up in the world.

The next month was full of struggle for Susan in managing her cook so that she doesn't gossip around in the neighbourhood, managing her office work and clients, grooming David and ensuring her parents don't visit her soon.

David was completely dependent on Susan, though he learned to complete many of his activities himself when Susan was not around in the house.

A strange unusual bond developed between them. For David, he developed a trust and faith in Susan, clinging to her the moment she returned from work. For Susan, her mind was overpowered with concern for David, when she had to be outside attending her office and clients. She stopped attending parties and somehow managed her friends with some excuses.

"What would have happened to David if I had left him that night? What would have been his fate if I had not sheltered him that night?"

Susan wondered, observing David playfully explaining to her what he did throughout the day. She felt satisfied that she had saved David from the unknown dangers which might have engulfed him that night. She smiled at herself and stroked David's hair, to which he responded with a childish grin.

The First Confrontation

It was a pleasant Sunday morning and Susan was humming one of her favourite songs. David was busy operating a solar robot which Susan had purchased for him.

Susan's mobile phone started ringing. She was familiar with the ring tone she had set up especially for the incoming calls from her mother's mobile.

"Yes mother, coming," said Susan gleefully. "Hello mom. Good morning, and how are you?" answered Susan to the phone call in a lively voice. The smile on her face suddenly vanished. "Okay mom, sure mom. No problem at all," she replied in a shaky voice and kept down the phone.

Susan's cook, Dora, noticed her tensed face and enquired, "Any problem, madam? Is everything alright? Are your parents fine?"

"Oh! Dora, I am so confused now. My parents are coming next week. I don't know how they will react once they see David inside the house. I hope they do not create a frantic situation. David has improved a lot and any unusual reaction may affect him badly. I am so afraid and worried," replied Susan with a tense tone.

"But madam, you need to understand that your parents will come one day or the other to visit you. You have to explain to them. You have taken such a courageous step to help David. I sincerely hope you will be able to overcome this as well. Let me know madam if I can be of any help," Dora tried to assure Susan.

"Thank you so much, Dora. Let's hope for the best," sighed Susan.

"Madam, let's pray to God. When I had seen David, I also had been sceptical. But looking at David's mental situation and his innocence, I have also understood how much affection and care he needs. You have been a marvellous guide and support for him. I am sure your parents will also understand," reassured Dora.

"Your encouragement is so precious, Dora. You are a darling," said Susan lovingly.

One week passed, on Sunday afternoon a car screeched to a halt near Susan's house. Susan went outside to greet her parents. They hugged each other with affection.

"Come, mom, come dad. You must be very tired with the journey," smiled Susan, trying to hide her worry.

Susan's parents entered the house and sat on the sofa in a relaxing mood. "Let me bring some water for you. You sit and calm yourself," said Susan as she went to fetch water for her parents.

"How is your work going on, Susan? Did you come across any interesting patients? You speak very less nowadays on the phone. Are you having any problems or is there too much workload?" enquired Susan's father, opening up the newspaper.

Suddenly Susan's father felt a tap on his hand and looked at her mother. "What's the matter?" He looked at her astonished face and turned forward to check what she was looking at.

Standing in front of them was David with the solar robot in his hand and fearful eyes.

Susan had filled up two glasses with water and was entering into the living room when she almost froze at the sight of her parents glaring at David surprisingly.

An unknown silence prevailed inside the living room.

Do I Love You?

"Susan, may we know who this is? And what is he doing inside the house?" queried Susan's mother in a commanding tone.

"He doesn't seem to be normal. Is he one of your patients? If that is so then why is he not at his home or the hospital? Can you please explain to us?" asked Susan's father in an equally commanding tone.

David was completely confused, unable to guess the whole situation and the reason behind the silence and grimness inside the house. He looked at Susan and tried to grab her attention. Susan's eyes were focused on her parents, unaware of David's fearful stare.

Dora was cooking in the kitchen when she overheard Susan's parents. She quietly came out and held David's hands to take him inside his room. She knew Susan has to now confront her parents and David must not be a part of it.

"Mom and dad, let me explain to you. I know you are very surprised. His name is David and he is mentally challenged. He came down one evening at my doorstep." Slowly and steadily Susan narrated the story of David and how she had decided to help him overcome his poor situation.

Susan's parents silently heard the whole story without any comments.

"Understand that you are trying to be good, my dear. But you are young and you need to have a life of your own. You have a decent profession at your disposal. After a few years or maybe even now, you need to find yourself a respectable man and get married," explained Susan's father.

"He cannot stay here, Susan. You have so many patients. Just treat him as one of your patients. Why are you suddenly so affectionate for him? Understand he doesn't have a house to stay in. Let us help him get associated with any decent social groups we know of, helping mentally challenged people. And most importantly you never discussed with us before such a big decision," said Susan's mother with her voice full of concern.

"I am sorry, mom and dad, that I did not inform you. I knew you would not appreciate my decision. David now has become too dependent on me and he may not be able to adjust anywhere else. He needs constant care and attention," Susan tried to explain.

"Are you in your senses, Susan? Don't you understand it will have a serious impact on your future life? Will any guy like to be with a lady staying with a mentally challenged person? Will you bear David throughout your life? Or have you already planned to carry on with your life with David? Can you please explain?" Susan's mother started losing her temper.

"Mom, I have not thought of my future yet. All I know now is that I have to support David, else the world outside will tear him apart. As a human being, I cannot allow that. My conscience will not permit that." Susan's voice sounded adamant.

"Ah! This is completely disappointing," uttered Susan's mother.

"Hold on. Both of you cool down," said Susan's father, trying to take control of the situation.

"Susan, my dear. You are very intelligent and smart. And you know how much we are proud of you. Please try to understand your mother's concern. She is worried about your future. She wants you to lead a normal life and not get overburdened with a mentally challenged person at such a young age." Susan's father stroked his daughter's hair lovingly.

Just as Susan thought of countering her parents, a sound of small steps approaching the living room caught their attention.

David was walking silently towards them slowly and silently. He placed himself at one corner on the sofa. Bending his head with a trembling voice, David started speaking.

"H...H...Hello Uncle. H...H...Hello Aunt. How are you? M...M...My name is D...D...David."

Susan stared at David, astonished at David's smartness in greeting her parents. She started wondering what was going on inside David's mind. The first time she observed David overcoming his shyness and trying to speak on his own.

David went on.

"I...I...know how to eat. I...I...know how to water the p...p...plants in the garden. I can c...c...clean the house properly. I can wear my c...c...clothes by m...m...myself. Do...Do...Dora has taught me to c...c...cook. Not all, not all, not all. I can r...read and w...write on my own. S...S...Susan, S...S...Susan taught me. I...I...I will take c...c...care of S...S...Susan. I...I...I will n...n...never, no no never hurt her. Give, give, give me a few days. I...I...I will find a j...j...job and a h...h...house and go away. Yes, yes, yes I...I...I will go away. S...S...Susan will get a h...h...handsome man. She, she, she will make you p...p...proud. Don't, please don't, don't, don't be s...s...sad with me. Please, p...p...please, p...p...please." With half-broken words David finished his conversation.

Dora could not control her tears and vanished into the kitchen wiping her eyes so that she was not noticed.

Susan was spellbound, she wanted to run and enfold David in her hands. Her heart was overwhelmed with emotions. But she controlled herself as she was worried about her parents' reaction. She waited with patience, clasping her hands in tension. The awkward silence in the room disturbed her, but she decided to wait.

A lovable touch on his shoulders took David by surprise. It was Susan's mother. She was standing beside David. David hurriedly got up and tried to flee. Susan's mother held his hand. "Don't be afraid, son. I am like your mother. Come here and sit beside me."

Susan was astonished to hear her mother speaking in a completely different tone. Her tension seemed to ease a bit.

"Son, you are a jewel. Your eyes are so innocent. Your words are endorsed with simplicity. You have made me so emotional today. Sorry for using harsh words against you. You don't have to go anywhere. You will stay with us as our family. If ever Susan needs to go out of town for work, we will be there with you. Don't worry at all son." With all her love and affection Susan's mother hugged David tight.

Tears rolled down her wrinkled face and she smiled. David nodded his head and smiled like a kid.

Meanwhile, Susan's father, who was silently observing David, came near him. He stroked David's hair and patted his back. "Young man, after so many years you made me cry like a baby. All along Susan had told us about her patients, their behaviours and how she cured them. We thought them to be just ill and not completely fit for society. We were so wrong. The innocence and purity within you are amazing and unparalleled. Now come on, show me the solar robot, I want to see that."

David jumped up like a kid, his face beaming with excitement, and went to bring his solar robot. He stopped momentarily and glanced at Susan with a smile. The smile was adorned with pure love and gratitude. Susan's heart melted in emotion as she went and hugged David tightly in her arms.

"I…I…I like you. Like, Like, you. Susan is good, Susan is good." David's innocent voice engulfed Susan with unlimited happiness.

"You fool, how could I ever spend a day without you. You were thinking of leaving me and renting a house. Never dare to think about that. Do you hear me? You are in my heart always and no one can take that away from me. I love you, David. I love you," Susan cried like a baby.

"Now go and show dad your creation. Go and bring in your solar robot. Or else the day will be spent in tears." She pushed David to go inside his room.

David ran like a kid to find his solar robot. He hurriedly brought it into the living room and started displaying it. Susan's parents happily played with him, laughing and giggling.

Susan silently observed them and wondered, "What if I had decided that day not to accept you? I would not have witnessed life to be so beautiful today. I am indebted to you God, my Almighty, to give me the strength and courage on that auspicious evening."

Susan's heart had said that day, "Let me love you the way you are?"

Short Story by Chinmay Chakravarty

Remnants of a Hope!

"What are those infernal insects called? Fruit flies or a more inclusive variety of the species of the small and bigger flies?" He does not really care to know the answer. He is only bothered about their nefarious activities. They are so tiny…like microorganisms…only that they are visible…else, they'd be very much like the virus that's been raging outside…threatening to come into the body any time…and this fear, this goddamned fear, that's been keeping him boxed in…perhaps for eternity!

He cannot help but be amazed at their dexterity: let there be any ripe fruit and any remnants of it, and they will materialise out of nowhere…swarming around it, noiselessly and with a purpose. Not only that…for that matter, any remnant of anything, any leftovers, from the half-eaten morsels of food left on the dishes to the dark red blotches at the bottom of the unwashed teacup…and they'll swarm over. Like black dots they'll be immersed in their existential task…you can easily wave them off…they'll fly away as noiselessly as before, but they'll come back again with renewed vigour. Want to kill them? No way, you'd only waste your time clapping your hands sans the celebration.

He looks disgustedly at the pools of them, busy as ever in his congested one-room tenement. His dwelling, he prefers to call it a cursed one, is particularly prone to their attacks: on the table with the leftovers on the plates; in the teacups on the floor pushed under the cots for action-to-be-taken later; on the fruit basket, even though that is mostly adorned by a solitary blackened banana; and almost everywhere in the place carved out of the wall called a kitchen and the floor-level gaping hole under it called a sink.

He smiles hysterically at the thought that he has to go out of the suffocating environs a few times during the day…a relief? Ha! Ha! Ha! Well, not for any darned activity, but only to respond to the inevitable calls of nature. And there too! The infernal insects dominate the community toilets that have been suffering due to the lack of the dedicated cleaners most of whom vanished as the virus started to surge.

He is also amazed at another basic aspect of his existence; he muses as he continues sitting on the soiled cot, inclining against the hard-rough cemented wall.

The apparently unsavoury attributes of his dwelling had never really been a disturbing thought for him earlier…when he worked for a restaurant which was frequented by customers not discouraged by the dilapidated building it was housed in, but really encouraged for its good food, and so, brisk business flourished from early morning to the late-night hours. The earnings were good. Handsome tips more than complemented his moderate salary. And life was good. His wife was taking very good care of the tenement, a home that he rented a couple of years into his job after leaving his parental place in the slums, and their daughter admitted to a good school.

The remnants…the flies…the visits…all were there, but somehow weren't visible to him. And then, the invisible flies came swarming in all around him, sickeningly visible. Everything changed in a single day…his workplace closed down…he got imprisoned in his congested tenement…infested by the visible flies.

For a couple of months, he continued getting his salary, and with his moderate savings life was not that hard. But slowly and inevitably, things took a turn for the worse. He got tense, rigid and irritable, boxed in against his wish. He also started noticing ominous changes in his wife's behaviour patterns: she seemed to have lost interest in cooking his favourite dishes; she too was constantly angry and irritated, pouncing on him for his immobility, saying nasty things about his manhood and so on. Her only concern that seemed to remain was that their daughter must get on with her online classes for which she forced him to part with his smartphone he so much desired in his painful confinement.

Suffocation and gloom only increased over the months as his house-rent dues crammed into the pending queue, their small television set went out of air due to the accumulating cable charges, and he could no longer order online his favourite items: from the readymade culinary delights to the cosmetics that were termed non-essentials in the wake of the invisible flies. Of course, he hardly had the money for these luxuries anymore.

He has now two growing concerns. Has love which has always been the pillar of their conjugal life been tossed out the window, forever, and that his lovely wife only hates him now? Would he ever get back his livelihood? He has heard that his restaurant might never reopen, because the dilapidated building is under active consideration of the municipal authorities to be demolished. Has he lost the whole plot in his life?

He blames himself on at least two counts: he never really cared for his wife, always leaving her behind inside that suffocatingly congested hole of a dwelling and never allowing her to do the odd jobs, like that of the most preferred one as a cooking-housemaid, and never even considered her demand for a stitching machine seriously, a job she said she was very proficient in; and he himself, too, thanks to his now-proven false sense of dignity and lifestyle, never wanted to do the jobs that were being recommended by his working brothers in the slums to sail through the crisis.

The hordes settle down on the table by his bedside. In a bout of fury, he claps his hands violently over them. The hordes disperse, but now are coming back to haunt his mouth and nostrils.

He sits quietly for a minute on his cot, thinking over something, with a stern look on his face. Suddenly he bursts into a flurry of activities. He collects all unwashed utensils and all remnants whatever or wherever they are, and starts washing; he takes up the broom cleaning all corners of the tenement; and he sprays out the remnants of a room-freshener bottle.

Raps on the door. He takes a satisfied look around his room, opens the door and sits back on the cot, sullenly as is customary for a traditional husband. His wife and his daughter enter. His ten-year-old daughter immediately sits down on the other cot, focused on her smartphone. His mobile! he thinks, not ruefully now, but proudly…lovingly.

The somewhat brighter and smiling face of his wife rather surprises him. Closing the door, she puts her bag on the table, and sits down on the floor by his feet.

She looks up at him and says, "My design of the mask is approved by madam, do you hear! From tomorrow she is calling me to her home. There she'll allow me to work on a stitching machine of hers and I'll get commission for every mask I make!"

"Congratulations!" he responds in a matter-of-fact tone. "I've also decided to visit my brothers tomorrow! We'll discuss the jobs that we can start with. Future is uncertain, you know! We must earn, and give a better life to our daughter and us!"

If she were surprised, she does not show it now. She puts her hands on his thighs, places her face there and cries quietly. He puts his right palm on her head, smiling contentedly. Suddenly he becomes oblivious of the choleric black dots.

Poem by Deep Wilson

Summer Breeze

Summer breeze

Summer breeze

In summer

Summer breeze inviting

On benches with us chatting

Looking around hill-tops smiling

Summer breeze

Summer breeze

Each day at the Mall, all strolling

Gaiety

In gaiety

All waiting

Enthusiastically chatting

Admiring

Evenings

Mall lit with smiles

Not an evening goes

When not a round

Even those from afar

Come in for a stroll

Never a toll

To be familiar

With all

Once on Mall

Can never be forgotten

In any part of the world

When a glimpse

Instantly joy abounds

'Hey, you were on Mall'

Then on

Greetings

Frequently come in

Connect

Without reluctance

Unhesitatingly

This be Mall's

Splendid

Gift to all

Summer breeze

Summer breeze

Aside a few

Whispering

Fascination

Through and through

Gripping

Endless rounds

Each morning

Each evening

Those at desk in mornings

Come in to refresh on Mall in evenings

Sit in café

Time and time surrounds

No time constraint

As all free

Not only

Shopping but

Meeting and meeting

With glee

Rendezvous

What a day

Never seen such

Anywhere

All know

Next morning

Clock at ten

All reminding

Their Pen

To fill

Accomplishments no end

This clock for years

Never failing

To make one pace

For years earnings

Where can one find

Such a time

Ace

To keep us all

In life's chase

This clock

Life's chapters opening

Each day a new page

So much to fill

To keep life on

Even when not to rush at ten

Pages open within

Filled years ago

To cherish

Every morning

At ten

These pages

Ever enlivening

With these

Never alone

Never in solitude

As countless pages

In all stages

Ever brightening

Every summer

From distant lands

All coming

Summer breeze

Summer breeze

Always inviting

Always reminding

To keep on

Overshadowing

That try tossing

Webs

Summer breeze submerging

At ten

At exact ten

Clock keeps chiming

All know

Our pages

Still opening

Our pet sitting beside

Admiringly looking

With all genuineness

Nothing to take

All to give and give

The world to know

What care is

Never anything to show

Never anything to boast

What a world

Summer breeze

Summer breeze

You have given us

Taken us to the world of care

Taken us to the world of unfailing adoration

What more from life we want

Those that say

Let

Presence matters

Yes, presence matters

Summer breeze

Summer breeze

Presence all around

That matters

Hill-tops with greenery

Keeping in freshness green

Every summer

Summer breeze

Summer Waves

What more from life we want

On Mall strolls in all gaiety go on

What more from life we want

We have our pages

That summer breeze turns itself

To show our accomplishments

What more from life we want

What company are we longing for?

All this is genuine

Stay with genuine

Summer breeze

Summer breeze

Keep speeding

Accelerate life's pace

Those giving way

While driving appreciate

A wave of appreciation here

A wave of appreciation there

Keeps life in all rhythm fair

Those who gel

Wish them well

Those who come in with a 'hi'

Keep them nigh

Open those pages

That give us mirth

From Ritz to Regal

To make life Regal

From one café to another

To make life fascinating

From one place to another

Summer breeze

Summer breeze

Reign supreme

Ascend victorious

Move on

Move on triumphantly

Glorious

Rise in magnificent high

With colour and song

Press on

Move on more vibrant

More strong

Onward press into mountain deep

Climb with vigour

Conquer the steep

Move on

Move on

Road no bend

Each step determined

Courage no end

Checkmate obstacles

Failure cheat

Sight success

Never succumb

Stay focused

Distractions numb

Accomplish

Top attain

With determination

Pocket glory

Always maintain

Summer breeze

Summer breeze

With you we grew

Childhood with friends around

Youth came in swiftly

With a mix of cordial company

In café

Smiles did brighten

Routine did lighten

Time and days flew

Moments around grew

Into the world of oneness

That brought in togetherness

Anxiety of what next enveloped

Youth bloomed in bliss

moved on

moved on

Fascination

Not to miss

Summer breeze

Summer breeze

On life's rounds

Merits

Work

Accomplishments

Recognition

Life's rounds each day

Inspiring

Sprint on

Sprint on

Don't slip

If trip

Regain

In your fall

Is your win

Sprint on

Sprint on

In genuine win

Gain just a smile

With a smile be healthier

That will keep you wealthier

Look for this gain

You taught us

Summer breeze

Summer breeze

Expressions come in

With all emotions

Through formal or informal names

Through our formal name

Success wins

Through informal name

Togetherness grins

What stays on

Both

Stay with

What is genuine

Togetherness wins

Summer breeze

Summer breeze

Give us company

With your gentle breeze

Keep us all in ecstasy

Don't turn

From

Gentle breeze

To Dust-storm

Don't entrap

In whirl-wind

Stay on

Stay on

With gentleness

Echo

Without utterances

Such be

Your frequency

To take nothing

To hold each hand

A child to grow

With breeze of oneness

With breeze of fondness

With breeze of respect

For all

For parents

Unconditional love

Where can we find such

Amazing world

Summer breeze

Summer breeze

Keep us steadfast

Through summer breeze

Show us

Not just hill-tops

But mountains

Of relationships

Summer breeze

Summer breeze

From Irwin Hall

To Halls of Fame

In distant lands

You never distanced

From giving wins

You never distanced

From giving grins

You stayed close

To numb all chills

You stayed close

To keep away

Dust-storms

Summer breeze

Summer breeze

We owe you a lot

What you have given us cannot be bought

We will not fail in taking your name

A number of times

As you have given us

All your time

Summer breeze

Your time to us

You have given

In plenty

This is what we all want

Time

Time that rarely

Each one for another finds

Summer breeze

You have time not for one but all

Timeless Elegance

Summer breeze

Summer breeze

With this Timeless Elegance

That you have given us in plenty

We can now climb

All steep walls

In just a jiffy

Summer breeze

Summer breeze

Essay by Srividya Muthuvel

Look and Learn

"Hey, knock-knock, what I am about to convey is... Oh no, please... I am not here to get convinced by your preceding notions as I have my own validations! Oh, come on... dominance isn't my objective darling... Ah! I am not sledging on to your flattered dice, honey!" Sharanya's commotion in accordance with her Intellect and Cardia were cluttering cumulatively until a prompt — "Discard," was pronounced by her Conscience.

Sharanya, A Teacher is rattling within in regard to elicit chronicity beneath — **Observe, Learn, Understand, Skill, Knowledge, Application** as all these factors conjure concrete base for the medium apprehended as Education. In order to endure the current simulation in education she encompasses and renders herself into the zone, by adapting and resonating as an acquiree. Sharanya now caters herself by imbibing in the incubation journey of human as a creature upon earth millions of years ago, while processing she recovers the procedures how humans extensively demonstrated themselves vigorously with physical factors and features present in the environment.

Preceding from Palaeolithic Age (Old Stone Age), humans had evolved in dire of inquisitiveness by demonstrating themselves with the present physical environment through trial-and-error method, where they did not plan the outcomes or objectives prior the action rather their actions were determined by the outcomes of their plan after its execution hence paving way to place and design the objectives attained through application. Stone Age man derived knowledge through raw and firsthand experience by himself through drawing conclusions in application of unknown actions (E.g: Rubbing stones with one another gave birth to an unknown element Fire, which was result of an application of unknown action) which facilitated him in sculpting his intellect with more minuteness by carving him from within. Sharanya's soul rejuvenates as she encounters the prime factor for learning — "**To Observe,**" which curates the essence of infusing curiosity in one's mind which frames "WH" Questions on primary basis for which both, The Vision and The Intellect chores in together to play in synchronisation by recording the visualisations that supports in formation of evidence through research, thus resulting in conclusion of the observation.

Sharanya now reflects that the children of the 21st century lack observation skills as they aredirected towards Rote Learning which hampers their Creative and Critical thinking, making them humanoids which unless programmed is inefficient for execution of any purpose, (E.g: In literature textbook children are not concerned in observing or even willing to know the name of the author, poet, poetess in order to be informed, rather they rote learn it as it has to be written in answers during exams as an Introduction of a lesson or poem), this leads to illiteracy even after being able to read, write and speak. To Improvise Observance skills a Teacher must facilitate the children – **"To Look and Not to Just See,"** as when they look they strongly observe and act upon their observations which results in concrete memory while when they see they merely reflect what they see which settles in abstract form that they tend to forget after a while as it has no reason to be remembered. Children must be taught to look towards everything with a purpose rather than an intention. To establish this, the role of a teacher is pivotal as he/she is responsible for shaping the mind of youths, (E.g: Children can be made to observe and analyse the genre, what a particular author, poet, or poetess concentrates upon. This will assist them to channelize their ideas and views which would aid them to recognize the writers according to their genre instead of just memorising them. Teachers must insist upon the moral given by the chapter or poem through the name of the author, poet or poetess as it's the writers who fill soul into the chapter or poem through their provoking thoughts but children merely remember the chapter's name and its summary but not their creator which makes the creation dull and cloudy even if it's enriched with optimism and valour.)

Sharanya pledges to induce Observation skills in children which will make them adaptable to build and reframe their imaginary skills as imagination renders ladder to reach the unconscious mind.

"Learning" is a continuous process as one learns from womb to tomb, with this proverb Sharanya dates back to ancient humans, their procedures, zeal, enthusiasm for learning and enlightening peers, leading to overall development across the zone. Learning leads to self-realisation proceeding to self-analysis enduring to allow the light of radiance to pierce and lighten the consciousness within which sparks the aura of divinity throughout conferring positivity in the surrounding. Primitively, humans believed in sharing their experiences in order to preserve and explore vivid and varied compositions of intellectual grasping in verge with nature and acted with utmost diligence in recurring it towards the expansion with rationality. During the phase of Palaeolithic Age, humans gradually learnt how to pattern and utilise tools like Sickle, Hand Axe, Scraper and many more through **"Learning By Doing Method" (Art)** that led to practicality for practice in deeper and scientific sense, this art was learnt and executed by everyone **(Artist)** as it served as chief need of the hour for survival which acted as similar interest for their existence. As the purpose of their living was alike (survival) no one had insecurities, rivalries, complexity or competition with each other as they firmly trusted in growing together and uplifting each other in the track to empower overall development.

Sharanya encounters with herself in present mode and analyzes the rank of "learning" in today's era, she discovers the inconsistency rate due to variations in the method of application to evoke learning as a prospect of inheritance for survival, by learning and practising that's been learnt **(Art)** for existence was replaced by glorifying the eminence of currency which disguised itself as the reformer of the nation vowing to deliver uniformity among the people by fulfilling their needs and wants, it manipulated today's human to get formal education which questions – **"Do to Learn or Learn to Do,"** that confines the ability, capacity and capability of the children **(Artist)**. Sharanya now frames her mindset to curate the Art beneath her Artists in practical mode which will embark their performance output in concrete mode through brainstorming, dwelling in the realisation, - "EARN (ATTAIN) TO LEARN (ACQUIRE), NOT LEARN (KNOW) TO EARN (COLLECT)."

"Understanding" demonstrates potentiality in humans since era, resulting in expanding the scope of being versatile exponentially, Sharanya elicits her soul and re-routes her mind to experience the zeal of understanding in humans during Prenatal stages (prior developmental stages). To understand, one has to surrender immensely in perceiving towards the acknowledgement of the agenda/product to be studied and analysed while experiencing it is the core phenomenon to sense by authenticating it through consensual terminal exposure (E.g: Earlier humans observed movements of the astronomical bodies, Sun, Moon and Stars which led them in engulfing the raw concept of Day and Night along with establishment of Time which they imbibed through the length of shadows that varied in a day according to the rotation of the earth hence by unearthing this they unleashed that day starts with the rays of Sun and the reach of its rays are not uniform as altitude of each place matters and acts as a prime factor in calculation of time, so they initiated to study and record the patterns which culminated through their analysis which resulted in inventing instruments like, Sundials (Day) and Water clocks (Night) to examine time). Humans' exposure inclined in interest with nature concluded in gathering experiences which they grasped naturally and applied for innumerous outcomes and updates, Sharanya relishes this acquaintance and vows to apply the essence of Understanding through sensing experiences instead of hearing and aiding experiences theoretically in books. Children of modern era have latest technology watches as their wrist band in order to follow the planned schedule such as, going to school, doing homework etc., hence by exercising time in this manner children must comprehend, "TO PLAN THEIR SCHEDULE OR TO SCHEDULE THEIR PLAN" in order to experience their outcomes in a conceptual and concrete manner.

"Skill" is the soul for existence of any form of artist as one roots and rises due to its exposure towards series of inceptions encountering the real paraphrase in life. Skill leads to catering information from sources around and explicit them by applying it in varied arena which enables and enhances their creative and critical thinking ability to the core. Ancient humans engraved hollow caves and built houses upon the trees to protect themselves from harsh climatic conditions as well as from wild animals, have we ever thought how this was possible for them with having any previous knowledge of carving or building? Well, Skill is an art which is inaugurated in pursuance with act enabling action that decorates and designs the structure towards its destination, our ancestors have carved sculptures on one single rock that mesmerises us even today, puzzling us about the inheritance of skill within them. Potters give shape to the pots through their skill by shaping and moulding them through their bare hands as their mind and hand believes in perceiving along with pursuing which means practising and reforming their own ideas every now and then. Sharanya's soul is enchanted by enduring such amazing cycle of psychology during that era's humans which lack for real in this generation children, She wills to instil this quality in her school children by making them identify and work upon their skills for proper execution of it. Children must be skilled to present their ideas propagating various dimensions, making their innovation much more applicable in real life demonstrations. Children must be engaged and imbibed with Life skills as well which would make them progress largely through performing live (E.g: In every vehicle, malls and buildings we have Emergency exit, making children aware and understand about their utilisation practically will endure them in resulting responsible humans).

"**Knowledge**" – Know (Perceive), Ledge (Share) is realistically important as sharing knowledge enlightens people's mind, soul and heart. Humans perceived knowledge about agriculture by observing the germination of seeds of fruits that they threw after consuming. When they understood the properties of soil which made re growth of plants possible through the seeds, they initiated this knowing by ledging it everyone around which aided them for permanent settlements around river banks.

The Principle: "KNOW TO LEDGE AND LEDGE TO KNOW."

"**Application**" – To apply the knowledge what is seen, known and experimented, paves the way for application of process resulting in various conclusions.

Today's farmers are experimenting with hybrid farming techniques taking agriculture in an advanced zone. Hence children must know, share and apply knowledge to experience

reformations and transformations exponentially!

The Principle: "KNOW TO APPLY AND APPLY TO KNOW."

As Sharanya was two-minded (*in ambivalence*) about show she would aid her children in analysing their real components in school, she now has a clear conscience for their exposure in real sense with application of naturality as an essence for every posture she would encounter! Sharanya's resonance has now been constructed with episodes of realism in physical world which would succour her in redeeming light in the young minds, hence Transforming them as Appliers rather than Suppliers!

About the Authors

Kiran Hiwale

Kiran is an IT professional who mainly writes project plans and reports but indulges in writing short stories and poetry in his free time. Ukiyoto has published his stories as part of three anthologies: *Abacus*, *Hanabira* and *Pride*. Unicorn Magazine also published his short story, travelogues and a couple of his poems.

Instagram: @kiranh26

Santhini Govindan

Santhini Govindan is a widely published, award winning author of children's literature in English. She has written more than fifty books for children of all ages, and her work includes poetry, picture books, short stories, chapter books and non-fiction. Santhini has been awarded two fellowships in Literature from the Ministry of Human Resource Development, Department of Culture, Government of India, for research projects connected to children's literature in India. She has authored and edited several English language readers that are widely used in schools across India, the Middle East and Southeast Asia.

S P Singh

SP Singh, an army veteran, is a novelist, short story writer and painter. His debut novel *Parrot Under the Pine Tree*, published in 2017, got shortlisted for the Best Fiction Award at the Gurgaon Literary Festival and nominated at the Valley of Words Literary Festival in 2018. His short story "Palak Dil" made it to the finals of South Asian Award for Micro Fiction 2019. Presently, he's working on his recent novel, *The Colours of Autumn*.

Priyanka Joshi More

Priyanka Joshi More resides in Pune. She is currently a college teacher of History. She does not have a literature background but she writes what she feels, penning down her emotions in words. She believes that "practice makes perfect." She has authored poems and short stories under a few publishing houses, but her dream is to author novels. In her professional career, she has recently been awarded Best Teacher Award 2022 by Asian Education Awards, KitesKraft; India's Top100 Researchers 2022, India Prime Awards by FoxClues and Highly Effective Professor award 2022 by HypeEdge Media. She also enjoys a variety of hobbies to relax after work. Connect with her on Facebook *@drpriyankajo20*.

Indrani Chowdhury

Indrani Chowdhury is a multiple award winning modern Indian author who now resides at Bangalore, India. Her poems have been published in various national and international anthologies and magazines. Her book *Raining Drops of Rainbow Verses* was published by Notion Press in June 2021. She was the recipient of Asian Literary Society's Wordsmith Award 2021 and Ukiyoto Literary Awards 2022 (Poet of the Year) organised by Ukiyoto Publishing. She was one of the winners of 3rd International Inspirational Women Award (IIWA) 2022 organised by GISR. She was also given Global Iconic Achiever Award 2022 by Priya's Wisdom Publication.

Kuntala Bhattacharya

Kuntala Bhattacharya is an IT Consultant by profession and a writer by passion. She loves to travel and meet new people. She has eight books published in her name: (1) *A Miraculous Discovery in the Woods* (novel), (2) *The Treasures of Life* (poetry), (3) *Come and Explore India With Me* (Travel magazine), (4) *The Indigenous Compositions* (jointly with other authors), (5) *Impromptu* (jointly with other authors), (6) *My Heart Goes On* (jointly with other authors), (7) *Wide Awake* (jointly with other authors), and (8) *They are Watching Vol IV* (jointly with other authors).

Chinmay Chakravarty

Award winning author Chinmay Chakravarty has been writing articles, news stories, short fiction and short stories since his student days and throughout his long service career in the media sector of the Government of India, and has also been editing news bulletins, books and journals. Chinmay has published his first book 'Laugh and Let Laugh' in 2017 and the book got a nomination for India Authors Award-2021 organized by NMCBI in Mumbai. His second book in pure fiction, 'The Cheerless Chauffeur and Other Tales', published in 2021, earned him an award as the 'Emerging Author of the Year—Fiction' in Literary Awards-2022, organized by Ukiyoto Publishing in Kolkata. He has published two more books on KDP Amazon in 2022, 'Funny and Fishy Tales' in humorous fiction and 'Humor Me: A Collection of Stupid Interpolations' in humorous non-fiction; both books being collections of his older blog pieces.

Deep Wilson

Deep Wilson is a prolific writer, author of *Beyond Lines*. Email *beyondlineswriters@gmail.com* to contact the Author.

Srividya Muthuvel

Srividya has been a passionate Teacher since three years at Sarhad School, Pune, where she believes in instilling practical knowledge for enhanced learning outcomes. She firmly believes that every child is unique as each one of them possesses variations in their area of interest which needs to be enriched along with academic curriculum. It will surrender them with the notion of being and getting acknowledged for their calibre which in return will invest their trust in a teacher, who acted more as a role of facilitator. Educating children never rests in completion of curriculum and preparation for exams, rather it is more varied. It reforms itself and makes provision of a stage that must be shared with the children by the teacher which will reciprocate the concepts in dual directions rather than being a monologue.

www.ingramcontent.com/pod-product-compliance
Lightning Source LLC
LaVergne TN
LVHW041843070526
838199LV00045BA/1409